THE MASK

James Murphy

In Between Books Publishing Company
Cedarville, California

The Mask

IN BETWEEN BOOKS PUBLISHING COMPANY
P.O. Box 300
425 Bonner St.
Cedarville, Ca 96104
contact: <juno@inbetweenbooks.com>
Cover art by James Murphy

Library of Congress Cataloging-in-Publication Data

Murphy, James.
 The mask / James Murphy.
     p. cm.
 ISBN 978-0-935430-32-5
 1. Spiritual life--Fiction. 2. Photographers--Fiction. 3. Mask makers--Fic-
tion. I. Title.
 PS3613.U73723M37 2008
 813'.6--dc22
                          2008039032

ACKNOWLEDGEMENTS
The author wishes to acknowledge and thank the following people, whose
presence made a positive influence on his writing: Duke Dugas, for the late
night discussions of all things mystical and profound, Joyce Hilton, who's
infectious laughter and humorous banter kept the hard editing light and
positive. Diane Littau, who's early encouragement and insight broke up
many writer's blocks.

*For 'seekers' ready to take off their own masks
and embrace an unconditioned, authentic life;
and for Fred who is out there somewhere—
turning the impossible into the possible.*

TABLE OF CONTENTS

THE MASK
by James Murphy

✳CHAPTER ONE

It was an unusually hot day in Seattle. All I could think of was throwing on a pair of shorts, a tank top, and getting outdoors. Who in their right mind would want to work on such a day? This was, after all, the Northwest. The sun could change your priorities at a moment's notice. Besides, it was Friday, when I could make time for a kayak paddle with a friend.

Like myself, John was self-employed. We met at Brookings Art Institute studying photography. While I continued to pursue photography as a living, John decided woodworking was more his calling. That was over 20 years ago and we continued to remain best of friends.

I called John to confirm a paddling time. "Hey, John, are you there? Pick up. Stop screening your calls!"

"David, hold on. Let me stop the recording. Okay, what's up?"

"The sun you fool, are we still on for a paddle?"

"In the afternoon sometime, I've just started a new cabinet."

"Tell you what, let's meet at Java Junky first, and I'll buy you an espresso. That should speed you through the cabinet. What do you say?"

"Sure, why not? See you there in half an hour."

"It's a deal."

Java Junky was a Bohemian hangout for artists, intellectuals, and free spirits. It had a cozy worn feeling to it, that allowed one to relax and socialize. Unlike Starbucks and the other giant franchised coffee houses, it was one of a kind. 'The Java' had tables, chairs and big couches scattered about in random order. Artwork, posters and announcements adorned the walls.

I arrived before John and ordered my usual coffee with a shot of espresso. I grabbed a local paper and headed to an empty table in the back. In the arts section, an announcement caught my attention: **Northwest Coast Mask Carvings at the Paul Corning Gallery**. I'd long had a desire to learn how to carve, but like a lot of other things I just never took the time to seek out a class or find someone to study with. Now seeing this announcement sparked my interest once again.

As I read through the article, I was startled by a loud thud! John had dropped a book on the table beside me.

"Be right back David! Just going to get my own espresso."

I glanced down at the book and did a double take. The title read: **CARVING A NORTHWEST COAST MASK**! In disbelief I picked up the book whose cover showed a beautifully carved mask. I was thumbing through it when John returned.

"Great book isn't it?" he said, sitting down beside

2

me.

"You aren't going to believe this, but I was just reading about a showing of Nor'   Masks. Look, right here in the paper," I ar   ting to the announcement. "I mea   's that? I've always wanted t   nd here you drop this

                                              ? I've had
                                                  shelf in
                                                  nd this
                                                  _u. I don't
                                              _o-who-whoo,"
                                              _ old T.V. series, *The*

                              u brought it, even if the Univer   _ said, laughing.

          n't think it's easy to carve a mask," John replied   _know woodworking, and this is more difficult than it looks."

"You know I'm not trying to create a masterpiece. I just wanted to get into it a bit; learn something, you know? Can I borrow the book?"

"Of course! Why do you think I brought it? Guess you're supposed to learn carving."

We made plans to meet in the afternoon at 3:00 o'clock for a kayak paddle. We walked outside together.

"I expect to see a finished mask since you were meant to get this book. See you at 3:00 then."

"I'm sure you will. Thanks."

The only thing I had to do that day was call my

editor and drop off a CD of photos. I decided to call from my car to double check the time of our appointment.

"Hello, Margaret Spark please."

"Sorry, but she was called away unexpectedly. Do you want her voice mail?"

"No, just tell her that David Murray called. I'll phone her back on Monday."

Now that I didn't have to deliver the CD, I decided to check out the Gallery with its display of Northwest Indian Masks. I went back into the cafe and copied down the address from the announcement.

The coffee shop was close enough to walk to the Paul Corning Gallery, a low, flat-topped building down by the docks. I peered through the large front windows. Long wooden benches were set back six feet from the walls, so people could sit while viewing the artwork. Various masks hung from the walls. The gallery appeared well lit, clean and spacious. Two gentlemen stood in one corner talking.

I opened the door and went in. Hanging from the inside doorknob were small bells that announced my entrance.

"Welcome!" The taller of the two men called out from across the room. "Have a look around, I'll be with you in a moment."

"No hurry." I replied.

I went to the first group of masks occupying one wall. They were beautifully painted with bright colors; reds, greens, blues, stark blacks, and whites. Most of the masks resembled human faces with a variety of expressions, while others were part human and part animal.

The most fantastic masks on display were the masks within a mask. Opening up a raven-like head I saw a human face nestled inside.

"Amazing work isn't it?"

I turned and was greeted by the man who welcomed me to the gallery. "I am Paul Corning" he said, extending his hand.

"Glad to meet you— I'm David Murray." I shook his hand. He was tall, thin, and handsome looking, wearing a tan colored sport jacket over a dark blue shirt. His crisp jeans ended in a pair of western style boots. His long black hair was tied back in a braid.

"Yes, the work is amazing," I agreed.

"Is this your first visit here?"

"Yes. I saw your announcement today as a matter of fact. I can't believe how many different masks are on display."

"I especially like Fred's work," he said, gesturing to a small group of unique looking faces. "They are so life-like, wouldn't you agree?"

I moved closer to the ones he singled out, inspecting their rich details and lively colors. One in particular caught my attention. It was very Asian looking. Compared to the others, it seemed plain, simple almost. Something about it drew me in. I felt the strongest urge to reach out and touch it.

"It's true, they seem like they could almost speak." I finally said.

"What do you think Fred? Can your masks speak?"

Paul hollered across the room.

"It all depends on who's listening, " the other man answered and walked over.

"David, I would like you to meet Fred Nowell. Fred, this is David Murray."

We shook hands and I told him that his work was very inspiring. A broad smile crossed his face as he looked directly into my eyes, holding my attention.

"I am glad you find them interesting," he replied.

He was a short man with a compact body, some-where is his mid- forties or fifties, I assumed. Standing next to Paul they were a study in contrast. Fred was neatly dressed in an emerald green shirt with charcoal pants. If it weren't for a bit of hair here and there he would have been completely bald.

"Are you a carver also?" he asked

"Well, no. Funny thing you should ask though, be-cause a friend just gave me a book on carving. I'm not sure if it would be better to find a class, or someone to teach me privately. Do either of you know anyone who teaches carving?"

Neither one replied but exchanged glances. There was a long pause, then Paul excused himself.

"Listen you two get acquainted, I have things I must attend to. David, nice to meet you. If I can help you with anything let me know."

"Shall we sit down?" Fred said, gesturing toward the bench. "Tell me a little about yourself and why you would like to learn carving," he added.

I told him I worked as a freelance photographer

6

and had lived in Seattle for ten years. My hobbies were kayaking and biking. As I talked he listened quietly, at times even closing his eyes as if picturing my words. I noticed that for some reason I felt very alert and energetic, and yet, at the same time, relaxed and calm. It was an odd sensation. Finally he asked why I was attracted to photography.

I thought about his question, telling him that sometimes it felt as if I had crossed over into another dimension, that my absorption in the subject matter was so complete I felt elevated to a higher level of awareness.

"Very interesting, could you elaborate?" he asked

"I can see the interconnectedness of things, especially if I am photographing nature. My mind even seems to slow down. Images I would otherwise miss just begin to pop out everywhere. I discover patterns and relationships that a moment before were hidden. Does that make sense?" I asked.

"When you have this experience, where do feel it? By that I mean, do you feel it in your body or in your head?"

His question was intriguing, but I didn't understand what he meant by head versus body.

"I am not sure how to answer that because it feels like the experience is in my mind."

"Have you ever thought that perhaps there is an energy in nature that is always flowing, creating patterns that our bodies can receive?"

"Sounds probable, I believe anything is possible."

"We also are part of nature and so can share those

same energies, but the body, not the mind, is what receives that energy. The body's experience is then recorded in the mind."

"So you're saying first I make contact with nature through my body, and then I think about it?" I asked, leaning closer to Fred.

"Correct. Because the exchange is almost instantaneous, it seems as if our minds receive it, but the body is what first makes contact with the energy of this world. The mind then attempts to decipher the information that energy contains," he said with a child-like expression.

"Hum. . . that's intriguing. Energy contains information huh? What sort of information?"

"Take those masks," he said, pointing to the ones in front of us. "They are much more than just carved pieces of wood and paint. They also contain energy and information. Under the right circumstances it is possible to access that information and know all there is to know about their origins."

"Their origins? Like where they came from?"

"If you have the time, we could try an experiment and you might get a better understanding what I am talking about."

I thought about his offer. I had the time, but what did he have in mind?

"Okay, what do I do?"

He got up and retrieved one of his masks from the wall. It was the same one that I had felt drawn to earlier.

"This mask, unlike the others in here was especially carved to hold energy. All you need to do is hold it in your hands, close your eyes, and do a simple breathing exercise I will show you."

"That's it? Just hold the mask and breathe?"

"That's all you have to do. Now, the breathing I want you to do is this: visualize the air you breathe is entering from the top of your head and going to the bottom of your spine, hold it there for a moment and again visualize it going back up and out. Go slowly and focus on just your breath."

"Sounds easy enough, then what happens?"

"After a short while you should start to see the mask appear. When it does, just continue to slowly breath and relax."

"You mean the mask will appear out of nowhere?"

He chuckled to himself, "That's right, and if it does, just observe it."

He handed me the mask, and at once I noticed a tingling sensation, as if the mask held a mild charge. Also, I noticed how light it was, hardly any weight at all. I started to comment on these things but he excused himself, saying I should take my time and that he would check with me later. Right before he left, he reached behind and lightly touched the back of my neck.

"Remember to follow your breath," he added, and then walked away.

I could feel a warm spot where he had touched my neck. I then held the mask and closed my eyes. Only darkness stared back at me as I imagined my breath entering my body and slowly leaving again. Time passed but nothing happened. I became very calm as I visualized my breath running to the base of my spine and back up. I was suddenly startled with the view of a grayish object in my vision. I watched as it slowly took the shape of the mask.

I could feel myself getting excited and feared it would make the image go away. I struggled to remain calm and refocused on my breathing. In moments, the mask was closer and larger, complete with color. I became totally engrossed in the scene before me. A strange sensation quickly spread through me. I no longer felt my body or my breathing. "I" was just awareness marveling at the scene before it, while at the same time I was aware of a "feeling" of panic lurking just outside this awareness.

I also discovered that I could move around the mask mentally, and view it from all sides. I went around to the back and saw only a dark outline of half a mask. I observed it in side profile, seeing the relief of nose, lips and protruding forehead.

Thoughts slowed down till I barely thought of anything. Then, quite suddenly I began receiving telepathic information from the mask. I "knew" that the cedar for the mask came from an island off the coast of British Columbia, I "knew" the colors were paints that originated from China, and I "knew" that Fred had indeed carved this mask. The knowledge was crystal clear.

My experience was shattered by the faint sound of bells ringing somewhere in the distance. As soon as my attention shifted, the mask disappeared, as if it were never there. Other noises intruded and in quick succession I was back feeling my body and breath again. I remained calm and then realized what had happened.

People entering the gallery had tripped the door-knob bells and were now talking somewhere in the gallery. After a while longer, I slowly opened my eyes and looked around the room. Two people were on the other side of the gallery, talking to Paul. Fred wasn't in sight, so I just glanced down at the mask in my hands, trying to make sense of what I just experienced. I now knew things about this piece of artwork that I didn't know before. I was still in a profoundly calm and joyous state when Fred finally appeared from a door at the back of the gallery. He looked over with a smile and nodded. After chatting with the new guests he walked over.

"By your expression I can see our little experiment worked," Fred said sitting down.

"That was the most amazing experience I've ever had," I replied.

Fred took the mask and replaced it on the wall. "I am afraid the gallery isn't the best place to be out exploring, sorry about the interruption," he apologized.

"But I knew where the wood came from, the paints, everything," I said excitedly.

He calmly listened, his hands clasped over his knees, acknowledging my account with nods of his head, while I explained every detail of the experience.

"But seriously, how was that possible just by holding that mask and breathing?" I asked.

He laughed and said not to dwell on the how, but to ask why it happened.

"Okay then, why?"

"The short answer is you were ready."

"Me? Ready for such an extraordinary experience?"

With a faint smile Fred reached over and gently tapped my shoulder.

"Perhaps if you could view your life up till now from a different perspective, then you would understand that this experience was just the next step."

My mind was flooded with questions right before he tapped my shoulder. Then the questions vanished and I returned to a calm state.

"What did you do, just then when you touched my shoulder?" I asked quietly.

"Sometimes it's better to feel into the body for the answers. You seem to rely solely on your mind. The tap brought you back to your body that's all."

"How do you know all these things?"

He looked amused. "That's not important. What's important is you had an experience. Remember you had said that out in nature with your camera you would sometimes go into a very different state of perceiving?"

"Yes, that's right."

"Well, it wasn't your mind that brought you there. It was moving your body around and perceiving through the body that did."

"Are you saying we shouldn't think so much, but just feel with our body?"

"The body has certain qualities that the mind lacks."

He just sat perfectly quiet with his hands clasped,

observing my reaction. I began thinking of what he said and before long was lost in thought. He got a big smile on his face and then it dawned on me. I was once again right back in my head.

"Okay, you talk and I'll listen," I said, throwing up my hands.

Fred said the body is always present, in the moment. Because it is in the here and now, it is connected and in sync with nature. Direct two-way communication can take place. Intuition resides in the body, not the mind; the same with feeling. The mind can then respond to what the body receives and make the right deductions and decisions about that information.

The problem occurs when the mind tries to "know" the world solely on its own. The only real knowledge is what nature, the universe and other dimensions express through us. The mind only stores that information. It doesn't produce it.

"So it's like when a person says, it 'feels' like rain today, or, I have a 'gut feeling' about something."

"That's right, they 'felt' it with the body first and then the mind deduced that it might rain. When I tapped you on the shoulder you felt it with your body and that brought your mind back to the present moment, back into your body."

"I'll have to think about that, I mean 'feel' that for a while," I said, still not sure exactly what he meant.

He seemed to take delight from my statement because he burst out laughing again, which caused Paul to holler over, "Stop having so much fun over there."

13

"I am glad you confirmed what my intuition told me," Fred said.

"How's that?"

"You said that you wanted to learn to carve, did you not?"

"Well, yes."

"I needed to find out if the mask would speak to you, which it did, thus confirming you have the potential to study what I teach."

"So you're a teacher? You have classes in mask carving?"

"That's correct, but what I teach is a bit different than just learning to carve a mask. The student works on himself more than a block of cedar," he said with a sober expression.

"How so?"

"Most people already wear a mask. It's the result of conditioning. Growing up, we are constantly bombarded with false assumptions on how the world is, how our bodies are and how our mind works. The student needs to get out of that conditioning. He or she must learn to move, think and respond in a fresh, unconditioned level of being, in a sense take off their old mask."

"If you take a close look at the carvings in this gallery, you will see fine examples of masks that reflect the best of Northwest Coast carving. The artist knows his skills and has great control, but they are just beautiful pieces of wood, no more. The mask you just experienced is a mask with power."

"Mask of power?"

"I carved that mask, as you know, and because it retained the energy that I let flow into it, you were able to have that experience. That only happened because I first had to discover my real self and let go of the conditioned self. My work is to help other people make that discovery also."

"I have so many questions right now. But one thing I can say, the experience I just had was real, and if what you teach is about that also, I am very interested," I said, eager to let him know the prospect excited me.

He folded his hands and gave me a long steady look. Then he said the best thing to do was to go about my business for a few days and 'feel into' what we talked about.

"I'll be here in Seattle for another week before I go north again, so maybe before I leave, we can get together again and discuss this further."

"A week? That's soon. Where do you live?"
"I live near Bella Namu, just out of town. I have a studio there. It's secluded and very private."

"Well, okay. I'll think it over and give you a call to arrange another meeting."

Fred gave me the gallery's number and I said goodbye to Paul. At the door Fred said I should listen to my body for the answer and not to think too hard about it.

I thanked him for his kindness, and for letting me experience his mask. Then I paused and asked him if his touching my neck and the warmth I felt had anything to do with my experience.

"Let's just say you needed a little energy boost to make it easier the first time out."

I spent the next two hours wandering about town in an aimless state. I couldn't get the experience out of my head: the mask, Fred, what he said about working on oneself. Yet, another part of me was very serene, I felt as though I was floating down the streets. It was like two states of mind competing for my attention. After an hour of this tug-of-war, an insight broke through.

It was my body that was calm and serene, completely enjoying a stroll around town, very much 'in the moment', but it seemed my mind needed answers to the incredible experience I just went through. I remembered what Fred had said, "The body and mind need to work together as a team."

I stopped by a park, sat down on a bench and closed my eyes. I tried to recall the mask but I knew that what I was seeing was just an image from memory and not the vision I had seen earlier. I followed my breaths in and out and became even calmer but couldn't go any deeper. Perhaps it was Fred's presence and the "energy boost" he gave me, that made it possible to have the vision.

Something about Fred convinced me he was a genuine teacher, a wise person, and that I could trust this person. His energy was very calming and loving. He even felt familiar, like someone I had already met but had forgotten where and when.

I looked at my watch and remembered my appointment with John. By the time I arrived at our agreed on 'put-in' location, John was already at the water's edge readying his gear. I wasted no time in unloading my kayak and getting my stuff down to the water.

"Glad you made it David," John said as I tied my gear onto the boat's deck. "I believe that's the quickest unloading job I've seen you make. You must have stopped for a double espresso along the way," he smiled.

"I had something better. I'll tell you about it once we're on our way," I replied, putting on my spray skirt and life vest.

With no wind the water was calm, almost glassy. I knew it was going to be a warm paddle so I first dipped my head in the water, then put on waterproof sunscreen and finally a hat. Our destination was a small island 45 minutes from shore at a leisurely paddling pace. Though it was calm now, the wind could come up suddenly and make for a rougher paddle back, so I took a few energy bars along just in case. Soon we were underway and fell into a steady paddle pace.

John maneuvered his kayak closer.

"So what do you mean you had something better? Don't tell me, you met some beautiful babe?"

"Remember this morning and the coincidences that happened, the book you brought and the gallery announcement?"

"Yeah, and?"

"Well, I ended up going to the gallery to check out the exhibit. The masks were amazing and I met one of the carvers there. I know this is going to sound strange, but we did a little experiment in which I held one of his masks and with my eyes closed did some breathing exercises that he showed me. Before long I actually saw the same mask I was holding and had this incredible experience."

"What! Come on, tell me the truth: The girl you met first got you stoned and you ended up at the gallery where you tripped out on some masks."

"Hey, I know it sounds strange—and no I didn't meet a woman. And you know I don't do drugs. What I just told you happened, just as I said. I even received insights about this mask, like where the wood came from, the paints, even the fact that this man Fred was the carver."

"Fred, his name is Fred? That's weird. Fred sounds pretty ordinary for a spiritual teacher like you seem to be describing. Are you sure he isn't a fake— some sort of magician or con man instead, and that you just happened to show up at the right time to test out his latest trick?"

It seemed nothing I said convinced John that I really had the experience I described. We paddled on in silence to the island and pulled our boats up above the tide line. After unloading a few snacks and things, we found some driftwood to lean back on and relax.

The afternoon was beautiful; a few puffy white clouds slowly drifting across the blue sky, taking different shapes before thinning out. Sunlight, reflected off the water like a zillion shimmering diamonds. John must have given my story a second thought because he asked me to explain more about my visit to the gallery.

"This artist Fred wasn't trying to trick me or anything. He said the way he teaches carving is to first prepare the student by giving exercises that bring the mind and body together. I am not sure I fully understand some of the things he said, but I felt perfectly calm and relaxed with him. A lot of what he described sounded like forms of meditation, or perhaps a form of yoga. I don't know yet, but John, the experience I had was amazing. It felt like I was in another dimension experiencing the mask."

"David, you and I are very different in a lot of ways. You're a seeker, you've always believed in something mysterious out there that calls to you. I am planted squarely on Terra Firma. I am not looking to find something. Life for me is my work and discovering better ways to do it. But because we are best of friends we have always accepted each other's differences. I mean even back in photo school you were into meditation and astrology. You seem to attract those kinds of people. Remember that girlfriend you had—the yoga teacher? She wanted you to go off to India to study yoga!"

"That's funny. I almost did it too, but I couldn't afford to leave at the time,"

"And do you think you can afford to drop everything now and go study with some guy named Fred? Listen, I believe your story about having some kind of strange experience, but if you turn 'New Agey' on me, you're on your own!"

"John, you'll be the first to know if this turns out to be some sort of illusion. I am supposed to give him a call next week, so we'll see."

"Well I'll tell you one thing," John said, gesturing

19

toward the sky and water, "*this* is no illusion. What a great day!"

✳CHAPTER TWO

The weekend flew by. On Monday I decided to call the gallery and make an appointment to meet with Fred again. I needed to know more and my curiosity was overpowering me.

Paul answered and said Fred was out, but had left word to say Wednesday around one o'clock would work if that was okay. I looked at my schedule and told him that's fine, I would be there. By the time Wednesday came, I was feeling increasingly nervous for some unknown reason. John was right, I had done lots of meditating years ago, but had drifted away from "sitting" for long periods. I always told myself that one day I would get back on track, but I never had. When I arrived at the gallery I started to go in when the door suddenly swung open, throwing me off balance. I sort of fell into the gallery, almost colliding with the person coming out.

"You must be David," the woman said laughing. "What timing, I should have paid more attention before rushing out the door."

"No, I'm sorry. It was my fault," I replied, after straightening up and composing myself. "Nothing like an awkward way to meet," I added. "Yes, I'm David. Have we met?"

Staring back at me with bright eyes and a wide smile was a tall woman with long black hair. I was totally captivated by her eyes, dancing and alive as they were. I found myself tongue-tied.

"I am Natasha, a friend of Fred. He described you well, said you might be stopping by before I left," she smiled, extending her hand.

"Glad to meet you," I replied. We just stared at one another for what seemed like a very long moment. Then I heard myself ask her if she had known Fred long.

"Oh, for a while now," she said, moving toward the door. "I really must be going, I am late already. Have to meet a friend. Perhaps we'll bump into each other again. Goodbye."

My mind searched for any excuse to keep the encounter going, but she was out the door and walking away before I could act. To my surprise I didn't see anyone else in the Gallery. They were probably in the back, so I just stood there for a moment. Then a voice inside said, *'At least get her phone number!'*

I rushed outside to see which way she had gone. I started to holler, but hesitated, and stood there just watching as she walked out of sight. I went back inside in time to see Fred come out of the back room.

"David, glad you could visit again. I hope you gave serious thought to what we talked about."

"Actually I am very intrigued. I thought after this meeting I'd get a better idea of what exactly you teach."

"Well then, let's sit down and I will attempt to make clear what is involved in my class."

It was good to see him and feel his presence again. His calm demeanor quickly settled my mind, and I was once again in a relaxed state.

At first he didn't say anything. He just seemed to be observing me with a faint smile on his face. As I was about to say something he spoke.

"She has remarkable talent. "

" I beg your pardon?" I said.

"Natasha, the woman you ran into coming in the door. She is one of my favorite students."

"Oh, Natasha! Right. How long has she been your student?"

He didn't say how long she studied with him but just said she was gifted, and that perhaps I would meet her again at some point. I wanted to talk more about her, but he quickly changed the subject.

"As I stated before, the mind and body need to work together, therefore I first give lessons that deal with body-mind awareness. Next, the student learns how to focus and direct his energy. If enough progress takes place, the student can then begin to carve, applying the knowledge he or she has learned."

Fred sat back and waited for me to respond. His brief attempt to make clear what is involved brought up more questions than they answered.

"I hear what you're saying, Fred, but what are the details, what are the lessons you talk about?"

A big smile formed. He knew I didn't get it.

"Well, let's just say you need to be rewired. Your present awareness level and your way of gathering information need to change. Each lesson is designed to make those changes. Before you can hope to carve a mask that has power, you have to understand how to obtain and express that power."

"How long does that take? How long are your classes?"

"It could take one month, one year or never. It is all up to how strong your desire is, and how powerful your commitment to learning."

"It sounds like it is more about self development than learning to carve a mask."

"Life is about self development if you embrace it, or you could live out the rest of your life embracing patterns and habits that just reinforce your conditioning."

I was starting to feel frustrated. I was used to having everything laid out so I could evaluate what was involved. Fred seemed more business-like than my first visit. I tried another tack.

"Okay, let me ask you this, how much does it cost and how many students are there?"

"The goal of my instruction is not money. Income from the sale of my masks is enough so I don't charge for what I teach. I only accept one person at a time to teach. Each person is unique, I tailor the lessons to match that person's inner design."

"When does the next class start, and where did you say you conduct them?" I asked, probing further.

"The class can start as soon as you are ready. My

studio is at my house near the town of Bella Namu in British Columbia.

He reached over and tapped my shoulder. "I know you have many questions, but some things can't be explained, they have to be experienced.

"I understand," I replied. "What would I have to bring if I decide this is what I want to do?"

"Everything is provided, you just have to buy your own food, pay for your own travel expenses and anything else you might want. You can quit the class anytime you feel it isn't what you want. If you want to begin this year though, plan on coming no later than October. After that the weather turns very wet and cold."

"You know I am going to have to give this some serious thought. I find it very intriguing, especially after the experience I had with your mask. I just don't know if I can arrange the time and meet your expectations."

Fred twisted up his lips and raised his eyebrows,

"Expectations? I gave them up long ago. I set my intentions in the present moment and then let go of them. What unfolds is what is right for me at any given moment. Because I accept what unfolds I am not attached to the outcome."

I sat lost in my thoughts, trying to think what I should ask next. On one hand it all sounded very interesting and attractive, a chance to explore possibilities. On the other, I wasn't quite sure what I would be getting myself into.

"Here is what we can do", he said. "When you decide if this is what you truly desire, then write and I

25

will send you the directions. It isn't difficult to find people in town who can direct you. I know our meeting has been brief, but I have many things to attend to before I return home in a few days."

"So when will you be back? I would really like to talk some more."

"I am afraid I only get to Seattle three or four times a year."

As Fred talked, I happened to glance over at his masks. I noticed that the one I had held was missing.

"Did you sell the mask you let me hold?"

"Oh no, that mask wasn't for sale, and now that it has served its purpose it is safely packed away."

Fred got up and said that he would write down his mailing address. I wandered over to his other masks, and wondered if they too were "masks with power," as he put it.

We exchanged information and said goodbye as he walked me to the exit. At the door I asked what purpose the mask had served.

"It got you this far, didn't it?" he answered, smiling with a tilt of his head. "Oh, and listen to your intuition. I am quite sure you will have the answer that is right for you."

In the weeks that followed, I tossed around my decision to study with Fred so much, I decided to give up thinking about it until I had a moment of clarity, or, as Fred said, my intuition would give me the right answer. Yes, I wanted to learn to carve, and discover more about myself. That would be a positive thing, but the commitment and time factor I wasn't so sure about. Then there were the "what ifs." What if he turns out to be weird in some way, or what if I can't get into his lessons? There I would be—stuck, far from home.

John wasn't much help. He thought I was nuts to give up a good thing here to commit to someone from whom I had received so little information.

"Come on, David, get a grip. You're not serious about this," John said, pacing about the room. "You only met the guy twice, and he just alludes to things without even presenting a curriculum or anything to suggest a serious class. Now you're thinking about taking off, for who knows how long, to be with this carver who speaks mumbo jumbo."

For some reason, John's rant had me laughing, which further agitated him. He looked out for his friends, and I knew he was concerned.

"Look John, I wouldn't even consider this if I hadn't had that experience with the mask, and felt a genuine warmth and sincerity from this man. I am no fool, I can usually pick up on hype. What if this is an opportunity that seldom comes along?"

John folded his arms and presented his best poker face. I knew he wasn't budging. His mind was made up.

"You talk as if you're going to do this thing," he said. "Do me a favor, okay? Don't go unless you are convinced it's absolutely the right decision. I would hate to see you get brainwashed."

"Don't worry, I'll let you know what I decide. Guess I shouldn't tell you about my dream the other night," I said starting for the door.

Of course he insisted on hearing.

"I was walking down a forest path. It was dimly lit, with shafts of sunlight falling in front of me as I walked. I heard crows cawing and looked up. Perched on a branch high above were two crows staring down at me. One had the face of the mask from the gallery. It startled me and when I looked again, its face was that of a crow. They then flew off, and the same one once again had the mask face. Is that strange or what?"

"You're right, you shouldn't have told me! Now I am convinced you should stay put!"

One thing stuck in my head that Fred had said: *'We are living out a world of conditioning.'* When I examined closely my own life, I saw the truth in his words. My life, for the most part, indeed, did consist of habits and patterns. I liked most of those patterns, but as I grew older I realized nothing new was taking place. What was missing was some inner realization that this life had a profound meaning beyond the mundane, beyond my own comfortableness.

Even though I lived the way I wanted, and to a certain extent, had a satisfying life, I knew deep down that something was missing.

I was single, and dating had become a hit and miss thing. I began to wonder if I was growing old too early. These thoughts occupied my mind when I decided to take a drive to the top of a nearby mountain. It was a clear and unusually warm night. I parked my car and got out to breathe the fresh air. The night sky was a grand display of countless points of light. As I gazed up into space, my mind wandered free, and I became humbled by the sheer enormity of it all. I felt diminished to a tiny dot and realized that my life held little meaning against such an enormous spectacle.

It was then I had the epiphany I was searching for. I realized at that moment, that if I went to study with Fred, I had everything to gain and nothing to lose but a little time. I got into my car and drove back down with the clear insight I was waiting for.

I wrote Fred and soon received his response with instructions and words of encouragement. As the time drew near to take the ferry up the coast, I gave John one last call. Like the friend he is, he wished me well and said if I needed anything at all to let him know. I told him if it didn't work out, he was to bring up the kayaks and we would have our own adventure. He liked that idea better.

✳CHAPTER THREE

I entered the ferry building with one large back-pack. My plan was to arrive early and beat the crowds. I was wrong. It seemed everyone had the same idea. It was the first week in September, and one of the busiest. The weather was usually great this time of year. Not only were there tourists, fishermen, and kayakers, but people returning from their trips to Seattle. I made my way to a somewhat vacant corner where I dropped my pack and then walked to the ticket line. I looked at my watch. It was 7:00 pm. The ferry left at 9:00 pm, and would arrive at Bella Namu around 8:00 the next morning.

Ticket in hand, I made my way back to my spot near the dock and plopped down next to my pack. I was starting to feel excited. Tomorrow a new chapter would begin in my life. As I mused about things to come, I happened to look across the room and couldn't believe my eyes! Natasha was standing next to the entrance. Without hesitation I maneuvered past the crowd. Our eyes met.

"Natasha, remember me, at the gallery?"

"David, what a surprise, are you taking this ferry too?"

I was so excited to see her that without answering I gave her a big hug.

"Yes, I can't believe you're here also. Where are you headed?"

"Bella Namu, that's where I live. And you?"

"Same place. I am going to study with Fred. I am really excited. Do you want to bring your back pack over with mine?"

"Sure, I have a return ticket so I am all set."

Just like at the gallery, I felt a strong attraction to her. She looked radiant. We sat down and chatted about the clumsy way we met.

She explained that she stayed with friends when visiting Seattle, and, like Fred, didn't make it there that often. She held down a job as a waitress in Bella Namu. I asked her how she met Fred.

"I'll tell you later, on the ferry. What made you decide to take lessons with Fred?" she asked.

"For a long time I thought about learning to carve, but I just never followed up on that desire. Then I saw an ad about the gallery having a show of masks and went to see it. That's when I met Fred and found out that he gave lessons. So here I am."

For some reason I didn't feel like going into everything that happened; my experience with the mask in the Gallery, the talks with Fred.

"Hum, that's all, just like that?" she asked, seeming to sense that more took place. I just shrugged my shoulders and smiled. She wasn't buying it.

"Okay, you can tell me the whole story later," she

said, smiling back.

The announcement came that boarding was to begin. Natasha briefed me on where to head once on board. We should move immediately to the top deck to claim a spot to sleep for the night. We made a mad dash for the top observation deck and found a place to lay out sleeping gear and back packs. Others were doing the same.

Before long it looked like a crowded refugee camp. Then we headed down below deck to get some dinner.

"Glad that's over. We should be departing soon," she said, sipping coffee from a styrofoam cup. Over dinner I asked her about Fred—if she thought he was a good instructor.

"You're the investigator type, aren't you, David?"

"I guess you could say that. I just like to know as much about a subject as I can before I get into it. Besides, you seemed to know him well enough. He said you were very talented."

"Is that so? He's the one with the talent, I am just a student like you."

"So you have studied with him?"

"Yes, but I only managed to complete two masks."

"What else did you learn?" I inquired, hoping she would talk about the lessons Fred mentioned.

She didn't answer. Instead she stared into her coffee cup as if words would somehow appear there.

"I know you are full of questions just like I was, but the answers need to come from Fred and your intuition, not me. What you're about to receive is a gift. I shouldn't unwrap it for you. I hope you understand."

Her words put me in a reflective and sober mood. The ferry was underway. I could feel the steady hum of the engines under my seat. I glanced out the window where hues of red and yellow light from the sunset were dancing off the ferry's wake.

"I can understand what you're saying. Guess I am just so excited and curious about this new adventure, and I know so little about Fred. Okay then, tell me about your life in Bella Namu."

"You're funny," she replied, "the investigator at work. I suppose I can tell you a little about Fred, I just won't go into his lessons."

I mostly listened as she described a Fred I didn't anticipate.

"Fred came over from Europe about ten years ago and settled in Seattle. He was already an accomplished carver and artist. In Europe, he happened to see a collection of Northwest Coast masks at a museum, and decided when he came to America he would learn from one of the best carvers he could find, in the old tradition of Northwest masks. What he focused on was learning the so-called Transformational Masks, masks with-in masks."

"Oh yeah, I saw a few in the gallery—really amazing things."

"Yes, they are difficult to get right. The masks were used in storytelling, social gatherings and dances. On the serious side, they were also used by shamans to cure people and converse with the spirit world. After mastering the techniques used by traditional carvers, he moved up to Bella Namu, one of the ancient centers for mask carving. What you should understand, David, is Fred was a yogic master before coming to America. He spent many long years learning to control his body, mind, and emotions. What Fred wanted to do was to apply his knowledge of esoteric yoga to mask carving and create a true mask of power."

"Natasha, I experienced one of those masks at the gallery. My experience was short because people came into the gallery, but it was an incredible experience."

"Sure grabs your attention doesn't it!" she replied laughing.

"Sounds like you've experienced it too."

"Of course. How do you think I got into carving?" she said, throwing her hands out as if she were welcoming in the world.

I couldn't help but laugh out loud. I was beginning to see another side of her, one that was lively and playful.

"Okay, so tell me, how did you and Fred meet?" I asked.

"I met him where I work, a cafe called, "The Raven's Nest." When Fred came to town, he usually stopped in at the cafe to have something to eat and a pot of tea. He was always polite but kept to himself. He had a small sketchbook that he entered things into; drawings, notes—whatever.

Some of the locals thought he was strange, just a

loner who lived out of town. I liked him though. His energy always affected me in a positive way. We never really talked much, but being around him put me at peace.

"It's funny how curious people can get. No one knew how he made his living. All they knew was that he was a carver. Some people even tried to sneak out to his place to spy on him. But before they could reach his house, he would suddenly appear on the trail and ask them if they were having a nice day. Of course, that made the rumors even more exaggerated."

"People in a small town get so suspicious anyway, but how did you eventually learn carving from him?"

"One day he came in as usual, but after his meal he showed me a drawing from his sketch book. It was a mask beautifully drawn and colored in. He asked me if I would like to see the real thing. Without thinking I just blurted out 'of course'.

"We set a date for me to come out to his place. At first I was all excited and made the mistake of telling one of my close friends. She advised me against it. *'Go alone out to the hermit's place? I would never do that,'* she said.

"I started having doubts, perhaps it wasn't such a good idea after all. Finally, I came to my senses and realized that it didn't matter what others thought. I had no reason not to go. I didn't tell anyone when the time came, and I kept our appointment. Fred had told me how to get to his place, and I had no difficulty finding it. He lived in a really interesting cabin and next to it was his studio. Directly in front of the cabin was a large meadow. Anyway, he was happy to see me, and after showing me his cabin, he brought me to the studio.

"Hanging from the walls were some of the best carvings I had ever seen. I thought my father was good, but these had the most amazing details."

"Your father was a carver?" I asked, interrupting her.

I must have asked the wrong question. She fell silent and seemed to drift off, as if her thoughts were suddenly taken from her. She fiddled with a napkin, tearing it into tiny pieces.

"I am sorry, did I say something wrong?" I asked.

"No, it's just that my father is a subject I don't feel like discussing right now."

Before long she continued, "I noticed one of Fred's masks looked like the one he showed me from his drawings, and I asked him if it was the one from his sketch book. *'Yes, that's correct,'* he said. *'May I show it to you?'* He took it down and brought it over to let me hold it. Right away I could feel something strange about it. It felt almost alive. I didn't fear it. In fact, just the opposite, I felt very attracted to it. I looked over at Fred and he was beaming ear to ear. He gave me one of those nods, which told me that he knew what I was feeling, that he had just read my thoughts.

"I remember asking him, 'Can I put it on?' He said, *'Of course'* and suggested that I lie down on the couch and just relax while wearing the mask. I could smell the sweet scent of the cedar. It fit my face perfectly, as if it were made for me. He said I should just relax and follow my breathing in and out, concentrating on bringing my breath all the way down to the bottom of my spine, and then up and out the top of my head.

"I did as he had instructed, but before long I became very sleepy. I didn't recall falling asleep but I was soon dreaming. I was in a meadow full of pretty flowers. I just watched them gently swaying back and forth. A bright blue butterfly came into view and flew straight towards me, stopping a few inches from my face. It remained there slowly moving its wings. The scene faded and then I woke up.

"I handed the mask back to Fred. He returned it to the wall, and asked me about my experience. I told him I had fallen asleep and described my dream. I asked him if the mask did that or was I just dreaming. He said the mask was showing me something, but that I woke up before I received the message. Then he explained that he accepts students sometimes to learn how to carve such a mask, and asked if I would be interested.

"I thought he was trying to be funny, as if his mask gave me the dream or something. Besides, I didn't know a thing about working with wood. For me, changing a light bulb was a challenge! Just to be polite, I said I would have to think about it, and I would let him know. Then I excused myself, saying I really had to get back. The whole experience at the time was too strange for me. I didn't want to hurt his feelings or be disrespectful. I got home and took a long hot shower while thinking the whole thing over many times.

"I thought that was that, but then I started feeling out of sorts, not my usual self. Thoughts of that dream kept occupying my mind. Fred came in a week later and for the first time I avoided him. I even felt somewhat afraid of him. I didn't discuss it with him, but went about my business, trying not to make eye contact even when I took his order. I knew he noticed my behavior, but he didn't say anything and was just his usual polite self.

"Then one night I had a dream. Once again I was in the meadow and the butterfly appeared. As before, it stopped inches from my face, only this time it spoke to me. Clearly it said: 'Once I was a caterpillar just like you, but I had to die so I could learn to fly. Now it's your turn to learn how to fly.'

"Something in my heart just opened up, and I knew that was what I was looking for: to know who I really was and what my purpose was. The dream was so lucid I woke up with tears in my eyes. I suddenly knew that Fred was offering me something that was a gift, perhaps a rare opportunity to change myself into something greater."

Natasha's eyes filled with tears. I gave her a napkin and then unexpectedly needed one for my eyes too. I wasn't sad nor was I happy, but her story touched a part of me that understood something profound. I too had always longed to know who I really was, but I had forgotten until she spoke just now.

There was a long pause where neither of us had anything to say. Finally I told her, "Do you know I just realized that I too have always wanted that same thing—to know myself, to know why I'm here."

She smiled and nodded her head yes.

"Can Fred show me that?" I asked.

Yes, she nodded.

We sat quiet for a long time just sipping our coffee and observing the other people milling around. The coffee was having an opposite effect on me, and I became sleepy. I told Natasha I was going to go lie down for a while. She wanted to read a book she had with her, and so I wandered off to the top deck.

My eyelids were heavy as I stretched out in my sleeping bag. The last thing I saw were millions of stars against the black night. I awoke suddenly, having drifted off to sleep. In the darkness people were milling around, appearing as dark shapes with flashlights flickering on and off. I felt groggy and then remembered the dream I just had.

Like my previous dream, I was walking along a path through the forest, and two crows appeared. Only this time one of them spoke. *'If you could see what we see, you would know that everything is energy.'* I must have asked them telepathically what that meant because I didn't remember saying anything. In my dream they answered, *'We are all connected by that same energy.'* That's all I could remember.

I looked over to the place where Natasha had deposited her belongings, but she wasn't there. I looked at my watch, I had slept for two hours! I returned to the lower deck. Natasha was sitting in the same spot, reading.

"Boy, I fell asleep fast. Have you been here the whole time?"

"I did go back to get another book, because I finished the one I was reading when you left. I saw that you were out like a light. Did you have a good nap?"

"Yeah, I had a dream that I've had before, I mean it was different but with the same birds in it. Say, what do you know about crows? Both my dreams had crows in them."

"Crows are messengers, and they can also shape shift."

"Shape shift?"

"That's right, change their form into another."

"Do you believe that?" I asked.

"I believe a lot of things that I used to think were just my imagination. I now believe that most anything is possible. Tell me more about your dreams."

I told her what I could remember about the crows. She explained that in my first dream the crow changed its face into the mask from the gallery to get my attention and that in the second dream their message was that we can communicate with all forms of life if we tap into the universal energy.

She said all this in a matter of fact way, as if, of course everyone knows this. Her short, curt reply reminded me of Fred's way of explaining things.

I wanted to engage her further. "How would you interpret the same dreams for yourself?" I asked.

She lowered her book, looking over the top of it and gave me an expression as if to say, 'Hey, it was your dream.' Then she continued to read her book.

"I would wait for clarity" she finally said, still hiding her face behind the book.

"Wait for clarity?"

Natasha put her book down. "Yes, dreams can be real. Only they happen in another space, you know, another dimension. This is why most people don't give them much credibility. We are so used to living in just this dimension that we can't access information from other dimensions. But clues will show up here, in our own lives, if we are present. Then we can complete the messages offered in our dreams."

I just sat thinking about what she said, remembering my dreams again, the shape shifting crow showing the mask and the message about energy. I pictured the two crows perched up on the branches.

"You're starting to like those crows aren't you, David."

"What!" I said, "Now you can read my thoughts!?"

Natasha stared into my eyes.

For a moment I was lost in her gaze, swallowed up into a dark mysterious pool of feelings. I had never felt so attracted to, yet at the same time, so intimidated by a woman. I could feel an immense power just beneath the surface of her calmness.

"Reading someone's thoughts isn't such a big deal once you know how," she said. "Most of the time I don't bother with it. People have such scattered and unconnected thoughts that it just comes through in a confusing jumble."

"Would you mind explaining how you do it," I inquired, this time giving her my complete attention.

"It works best when a person is being reflective, as you just were. What happens then is the mind creates thought forms that are sent out much like radio waves. Thought forms are a collection of related ideas held together in what's called an energy bundle. If I relax and connect to the person sending them, I can intercept that bundle and hopefully make sense of what they were thinking."

"So my energy bundle had to do with crows?"
"I am not finished," she quipped. "My intuition then breaks down that energy bundle into separate key thoughts. In your case it was "crows," "flying," and "forest." Since I had a neutral feeling when you thought those thoughts I deduced that you were just thinking about your dream without any charge attached."

"Amazing, because you're right. What do you mean by 'charge'?"

"Many thoughts that we dwell on have an emotional charge attached to them. This charge triggers the body to respond with emotion, whether it is anger, sadness, sexual arousal, or whatever. When I intercept their thoughts, I usually feel the charge that is associated with them and sometimes it's not pleasant."

As she talked I tried to listen and think about what she was explaining while another part of me wanted to touch her, feel her body, smell her scent. An attraction was building and I didn't know what to do about it. I decided to think certain thoughts with a strong emotion attached. I thought of how nice it would be to be kissing her and making love with her. I waited to see if she picked up on my thoughts. Finally I asked her.

"So Natasha, what do think I am thinking right now? Please take your time." I asked, holding her gaze to see if I could get my answer from her eyes.

"By that playful look I don't have to work too hard to understand your desire. Sometimes a woman doesn't have to read minds to know what a man is thinking!"

Clouds hung low as the ferry pulled into the old ferry terminal. Creosote pilings jutted out at odd angles, as the ferry slid between the best of the lot, moaning until it came to a stop. Passengers were ready to exit, standing as one big crowd waiting for the signal to disembark. Natasha and I were in no hurry.

We waited till the crowd thinned out before walking out onto the pier. The pier looked like it couldn't secure a rowboat. Walking along I noticed large gaps in the wooden planks that revealed the water below.

"Boy, how many lawsuits do they get each year?" I asked Natasha who was making a beeline for the street outside the terminal.

"Money is tight up here. People don't sue each other. Didn't you see all the signs warning people to stay alert? Besides we are lucky to have a ferry stop this far north."

I agreed as we said goodbye. She had to unpack and attend to things before working that night at the Raven's Nest. I told her I'd come in for dinner later.

I checked into the Cedar Inn, took a shower and a brief nap, having not slept much on the ferry. I spent the remainder of the day exploring Bella Namu, taking pictures and soaking up the scene. Bella Namu was a very old fishing village and was at one time a thriving logging community. It was also home to more than one tribe of Indians known for their carvings. Museums worldwide contained some of their famous masks. Old totem poles and some newer more brightly colored ones were standing like giant guardians throughout Bella Namu.

The air smelled of sea salt and rich vegetation. Giant trees grew thick at the edge of town. Moss clung to the wood of any structures that didn't get direct sunlight, or were abandoned.

I pulled out the map Fred sent to me and found the path to his cabin just at the edge of town, right where he said it would be. It was still early and I felt the strongest urge to walk to his house, but I knew I wanted to relax in town first and see Natasha before committing to the journey. I got the feeling that once I took that path, my life would never be the same. Tomorrow would be soon enough.

It was early evening when I entered the Raven's Nest. The cafe was crowded but I managed to find a table just as a couple was leaving.

"Here's a menu dear, I'll be right back," said the waitress.

I looked around and spotted Natasha busy with other customers. She looked so attractive I started wondering, for the first time, if she had a boyfriend in town.

The cafe reminded me of an old sportsman's

lodge. The walls were adorned with mounted trophy fish, the head of a heavily antlered buck, and off in the corner stood a full-sized brown bear, standing upright on its back legs—looking almost alive! The lighting was low, and a faint layer of smoke hung about. A pool table occupied one corner and large glass mirrors reflected the room from behind a well stocked bar.

"Just got off the boat today?" The waitress asked, holding her pad and pencil ready for my order.

"Yes, seemed like a quick trip from Seattle but this town feels far away from there. I'll have the salmon special. Say if you get the chance, could you tell Natasha I am over here?"

"Oh, are you a friend of Natasha? She's a real darling."

"Yes, we met in Seattle."

"What brings you here?" she asked.

"Well, I am here to study with Fred. Do you know him?"

"Fred! Oh my yes. Now *there* is a gentleman. So you'll be staying up at Fred's. Be sure to tell him Helen said hello."

"I will do that. Listen, my name is David. Glad we got to chat."

Helen reminded me of a favorite aunt of mine, not only in appearance (early sixties with a plump figure) but in personality too. Polite, but on the inside—feisty. She seemed the type to know everything that went on in this small town.

"Well hello, stranger."

I looked up to smiling eyes.

"How is it going Natasha? You folks are crowded tonight."

"It's always like this after the ferry comes in. Later in the week it will thin out, and pretty soon only the locals will be here. Did you have a good day exploring the town?"

"That I did. I even found the path that Fred had on his map. What time do you get off tonight?"

"Not till late. One of the waitresses called in sick so I have to fill in for her. I'm afraid I will be ready for bed when I get off. Besides, you should get to sleep early. Your big adventure begins tomorrow."

"I know. Just thought we could visit for a while before I left. But hey, let the adventure begin!"

Before returning to her duties she leaned over the table and whispered in my ear, "Tomorrow you enter Fred's world. Don't take it lightly."

❊CHAPTER FOUR

The day broke clear and crisp. After several cups of coffee and a trip to the general store for food, I shouldered my now bulging backpack, made my way to the trailhead, and took my first step down the path. I had only gone a short distance when I felt a strong sense of deja vu. Everything felt familiar: the narrow path, the low light, the smell of the forest. I'd never been this far north before, so I knew the familiarity was unfounded and a bit eerie. I put the feeling aside and walked on, falling into a steady rhythm. I noticed how abundant and thick the vegetation was, clinging to trees like jungle vines. A velvety carpet of emerald green moss seemed to cover every rock and log. The pungent smell of rotting wood filled my nostrils. The trail didn't appear to get much use. Vines were running across it in a determined attempt to reclaim their ownership of the earth. *'Surely, enough people take this trail to keep it trampled down,'* I thought.

According to Fred's letter, the hike to his place was to only take about an hour. After 30 minutes, the forest grew dark, the sun hiding behind thick clouds that appeared out of nowhere, and tall trees that lined the path obscuring the light. As I looked up at the towering trees, I tripped over some roots that sent me rolling over onto my backpack. I lay there a moment. *That's what I get for not paying attention,* I thought, laughing to myself.

But before I could get up, two crows suddenly appeared, landing on a branch directly above me, cawing loudly. At that instant I recalled my dream and a cold shudder shot down my spine. At any second I expected to see the mask on the face one of the crows. I waited, frozen in fear, but nothing happened. The two crows continued to stare down at me and caw. Or were they laughing at me? I caught sight of myself in my mind's eye as I might look to the crows cawing above me, and started to laugh, releasing the tension I had just felt.

"So you think this looks funny, do you?" I yelled at them.

They stopped cawing and flew off. After dusting myself off and adjusting my pack, I took off down the trail again, this time keeping a keen eye on where I was walking.

Before long I came to a split in the trail. One fork went off to the right, the other toward the left. Neither path looked more used than the other. Oh great, I thought, I get lost before I even make it to Fred's. Now why didn't he mention this or show it on his map? While I was puzzling over which way to go, the two crows reappeared, alighting high up in a nearby tree.

"Okay Mr. Crows, now what?" I hollered up to their lofty perch. Without even a squawk, they swooped down towards me. At the last second they veered off and

flew down the path to the right, their jet-black feathers shining in the diffused sunlight.

For some reason the answer was plain as day. Follow the birds! So I did.

I nearly jumped out of my skin when a voice sounded nearby.

"Glad to see you made it, David. Welcome." It was Fred, appearing unexpectedly beside a tree, a wide grin on his face.

"Fred! You nearly gave me a heart attack," I shouted as we met and hugged one another. "Have you been waiting here long? Are we near your place?"

"Oh just up the trail a bit. How was the walk in?"

"Fine until I reached the fork in the path, which I didn't see on your map by the way!"

"Good thing you followed those crows then. The other path would have taken you to the ocean shore, far from my place."

"That's right, the two crows—hey, wait a minute, how did you know about those two crows?"

Fred put his hand on my shoulder and smiled, "You have now entered my world. Outside rules don't have to apply here. This is where the impossible can become the possible. Let me show you where I live."

A short distance away the path opened up into a long meadow. Sitting on a hill at the end of the meadow were two log cabins. The larger cabin had a deck facing the meadow. I could see solar panels on the roof.

We followed the path through the meadow to the entrance of the first cabin. Inside was one large room with a stone fireplace and a towering stack of wood next to it. The ceiling had huge exposed beams supported by equally large posts. Skylights gave the cabin plenty of light. Off in one corner was the kitchen area with a small wood burning stove and a smaller stack of wood. Nearby stood a rustic table with four high backed chairs. Facing the fireplace was an oversized couch. A small desk next to the window faced out towards the deck and the meadow.

Fred pointed out two smaller rooms leading off from the main room. "It's not much, but it's perfect for me. This is how I like to live."

"Not much! Fred this is great. Did you build this?"

Fred explained that he found the place eight years ago, abandoned and broken down. The last occupant just left and never came back. People in town didn't even know who owned it, because it wasn't unusual for people to occupy or build on government property far from town in such a remote area. Fred said it was like homesteading.

Beside being far from town, rumor had it that it was the site of ancient Indian burials. No one wanted to live there anymore. Fred spent two years repairing the building, bringing in a generator and solar panels. He also had a large supply of deep cell batteries to store power. The land had a good well and rich soil for the short growing season.

Next I was led to his studio. Upon entering I saw masks of all shapes and sizes hung from the walls. In the middle of the room was a work table with various woodworking tools laid out in an orderly fashion. An old wine barrel, filled with water stood at one end of the table with large pieces of wood in it. The studio also had a stove and a well-worn rug directly in front of it. Four high stools were arranged around the work-table, with a couple of skylights directly above. I glanced outside, and could just barely make out a road almost covered over by undergrowth. It led away from the mask studio.

"Hey, is that a road out there?" I asked.

"That's an old logging road. It leads back into town, but it's a longer walk. That's how I got supplies to this place. It hasn't been used for years."

Standing up in one corner was a six foot log that looked like it was ready to be made into a totem pole. "Are you going to carve this as a totem pole, Fred?" I asked, smoothing my fingers along the wood.

Fred walked over to the log slowly, and gave it a pat. "This will be my first 'totem of power' someday. If you think a mask can hold power, imagine what this fellow could hold!"

Fred suggested we take some lunch out on the deck. He showed me the room I was to use, and said I could unpack and get settled in later, that we had things to discuss first, over lunch. I took a seat outside on the deck overlooking the meadow, a field of late blooming blue flowers.

Blue flowers . . . I thought of Natasha's dream. Fred soon appeared with cheese, bread and tea.

"Hey, you won't believe who came over on the same ferry with me," I said, munching on the food.

"Natasha."

"How did you know?"

"By the look on your face, who else would it be?" Fred answered, sipping his tea.

"You're right. She is an amazing person. She did mention that she was a student of yours. How long ago was that?"

"She still is."

"Really?"

Fred didn't say anything, just sipped his tea. Then he looked at me with a clarity that made me self-conscious. I suddenly felt clumsy eating and put the piece of bread and cheese down. I had never seen such a fierce look from him before. It wasn't an angry or vindictive look, just a focus that shot straight through me. I gazed out at the meadow, not knowing what to say next.

"Some journeys take a long time, which brings us to yours," he finally responded.

I looked back at him and his eyes were now soft, lifted up by his smile.

"You've gone through a door, and that door has closed. If you open it again and walk back out, it might be some time before you discover how to find it again, so I would advise you to walk the path that has opened up for you."

I just nodded and sipped my tea. For the next hour or so Fred explained that I would follow a daily routine that would build up a new momentum. Once that momentum was established, I would find it easier to concentrate on the lessons that he would give me. As he talked I began to notice a strange thing take place. When a question popped into my head, he would answer it immediately. I didn't have to ask it. I wondered what he meant by momentum. In the very next sentence he addressed it.

"When we practice something over and over again, our actions establish a habit, which in turn creates a pattern. Once that takes hold, a momentum builds up that strengthens the pattern. Then all we have to do is think about the habit or action, and energy is sent through the pattern, inviting us to act it out."

I remembered Fred saying that I needed to be rewired when I saw him at the gallery.

"You bring with you, David, all the conditioning and habits that make up your life at this moment. As I said before, you first need to be rewired, to establish a new set of patterns that, through practice, will build a new momentum. Once your momentum is strong enough, you will be able to follow this path without falling back into old patterns of behavior."

I wondered where the path led.

"This path leads to self-awareness and your true inner self." Fred said, apparently reading my mind once again.

He said I should go now and unpack, take a rest, and we would meet in the afternoon for my first lesson.

My room was spare but seemed to have everything necessary for an extended stay. The bed was a firm futon with a few wool blankets. There was a mirror over the sink; a sink which had no running water. The water came from the well outside by the buckets full. A large pail was on the floor next to the sink. A small writing table and chair took up the space in front of the window. One large drawing on the wall looked Tibetan. It was a mandala of sorts, a colorful diagram that resembled the energy centers that run up and down the body. A small closet was where I put my unpacked backpack.I stretched out on the futon and drifted off to sleep.

A chopping noise woke me up. I looked out my window to see Fred swinging a double-bladed axe, neatly splitting rounds of wood with one blow. I got up and went outside.

"I assume that's the outhouse," I said, pointing to the tiny hut set up on a platform.

"You would be right," he replied. "It's a great working composting toilet. Of course you'll need a flash-light at night."

I sat and watched Fred swing the axe. His move-ments were that of a twenty-year-old in top shape. There was no wasted movement, and the axe found its mark every time. He must have split a half cord before he stopped and he wasn't even breathing hard or sweating.

"You can sure split wood," I told him.

"The axe and I have an understanding: it does its job and I do mine. I always make sure it stays sharp and clean. Tools are like that, they need to know you care about them. Then they will serve you well. Okay, let's go to another work area, one where we split the truth from the false."

After a brief walk past the meadow and through a

stand of large hemlocks, we arrived at a small clearing. Facing us was a grove of medium sized cedar trees. The cedars formed an almost perfect circle. It was quite amazing. I realized we were surrounded by trees; giving the place a cathedral-like appearance.

"What a beautiful space Fred. It feels ethereal."

"Special, yes. The energy here is very focused. It wants to draw you up into the sky. Feel it."

He was right, I just felt like staring up into the sky.

"This is where you will come each day, no matter the weather. This is where you will check in with yourself.

"Check in?" I asked.

He explained that when we wake up from a night of sleep, we must consciously reestablish our connection with our own inner energy force. If not, then that energy will immediately start to run through our established patterns and we lose the chance to set our intentions for the day, intentions that can create new energy patterns. Once our new intentions are set, we can then listen to what our intuition is trying to tell us. Our intuition knows what we need at any given moment and it knows how to respond to that moment.

He further stated that each morning, I should first meditate on my breathing as I did in the gallery. Visualize the breath coming in from the top of my head, down to the base of my spine, then up and out the top again.

"Hidden within the simplest action is profound truth," Fred said, pointing toward the cedars. "I want you to simply walk to those trees and back again."

I did as he instructed. "So what did you discover

on your way there and back?" he asked me.

"Ahhh, discover? Was I supposed to discover something?"

"Only if you were paying attention. Don't assume anything. Always keep your antenna up. Try again."

This time I went slower, trying to be more aware. On returning I told him I heard the chirping of birds and I felt a slight breeze moving across the clearing.

"Okay, better. Now I want you to feel your feet as you do this, feel each step."

When I returned I told him that I was concentrating on my feet but didn't notice anything different this time, maybe because my attention had been occupied with my feet.

My report had Fred laughing so hard that I laughed too. After we calmed down, Fred explained that by putting attention on my feet, I would move out of my head and into my body. "This simple act will center and ground you. The awareness you need resides in your body, not your mind. With practice, you will be able to sense your surroundings with your body. "Watch me," Fred said, "and notice I have my eyes closed."

Fred walked straight to the trees, stopped a foot away, turned and walked back. He seemed to hardly touch the ground; it was more like he floated to the trees and back, all the time with eyes shut. It was hard to believe he knew when to stop in front of the tree, and actually walk a straight line there and back. "Now you try. Just tune into your body's sensing abilities,"

I gave it a try, but couldn't help opening my eyes

once I crossed the clearing. I just knew I would bump into the trees. Also, I wandered off course. My mind was too present to listen to my body, even if I knew what I was supposed to listen for.

Fred was kind, saying it takes practice, and not to get discouraged. I had to learn to walk before I could expect to run.

Next, Fred brought out a blindfold and a pair of earplugs.

"These are your training wheels. With sight and hearing gone, your mind will only have smell, touch and taste to distract you with."

"Distract? I thought our senses are what we depend on to make our way in the world."

"They are, but nature is also sending out signals, vibrations if you will. Use your body not your mind to receive nature's signals. You will learn to trust your body and not be distracted by your mind," Fred said. He went on to explain that as we develop more awareness, we also increase the rate of our own vibratory frequency.

"People attract things to them in a number of ways. One way is by this vibrational signal that we send out. If our signal is in the lower spectrum, then we will attract things that vibrate at that lower rate. The important thing to remember is that our emotions can change our signal too. So if we have a habit of becoming angry, we will often attract people who will feed off that energy. Likewise, if we vibrate at a higher level, we will attract people and things that are beneficial. Nature vibrates at a higher level than most people are aware of, but with practice we too can match it's frequency and then communicate our thoughts and energy in more profound ways. If we want to make real contact and communicate with different aspects in nature, we must learn to not only increase our own vibratory rate, but also learn to adjust to nature's."

Fred told me to put on the blindfold and ear plugs, and he would lead me around close to various objects so I could get an idea what he meant.

I asked him if this had anything to do with learning to carve a mask, which was the reason I came here.

"It has everything to do with it. You need to feel the wood and the carving tools with your body. How else can they speak to you?"

It seemed a bit farfetched, but I decided not to voice my doubts, especially when he was my only eyes and ears just then.

As Fred slowly led me around the clearing, I tried to "feel" anything different. Instead, I felt slow and clumsy, soon becoming hopelessly disoriented. My mind kept thinking how foolish this whole thing was when I suddenly felt a gentle knock to my head.

Fred pulled down one side of my ear muff, "Get out of your head! Feel here," he said, tapping me just above my stomach, a little to the left.

I did as he suggested and we continued on. I put all my concentration on the spot he had tapped. Time seemed to slow down, I became aware of my breathing. I felt centered in that one spot Fred had tapped, as if my entire awareness was now centered there. Then I detected something that felt like a pressure or wave at the location of my focus. I could "hear" a slight humming sound that seemed to get louder as the wave pushed against that spot.

Suddenly, the pressure became very strong and the hum grew distinct. We stopped moving and Fred took off the blindfold. Wow! I was standing right in front of the trees.

"I don't believe it Fred! I could actually feel it and hear it."

Fred motioned me to take off the earmuffs. "You don't have to shout," he said, laughing.

"What was the sound I heard? It got louder with this pressure I felt."

"The pressure, as you put it, is the tree's energy signal being broadcast out in all directions. Everything that vibrates also has a sound that we can receive with our 'inner ear'. The center in your body that I tapped is your receiver. You will learn to adjust your receiver to intercept very different wave forms. For now you did good. It's a start."

"A start! I felt like I could actually feel the trees."

"Of course you could. Imagine being able to feel all of life around you, but without proper training you would go crazy! It would be like putting a million volts thru a 110 wire. Everything would blow!" Fred said, throwing out his arms to make the point.

"Come to think of it, you're right. You mean everything out here is vibrating, and has sound to it?"

Fred reached over and tapped me on the head,

"Isn't that what I've been saying?"

Fred picked up a small stone and handed it to me. "Throw this up into the air and catch it."

I gave it a toss and reached out and caught it when it came down.

"Simple eye and hand coordination, right?"
"Of course, every kid learns that."

"Now that you have discovered a place in you that can sense your surroundings, use it to catch the falling stone," Fred said, handing me the blindfold.

"Hey, I just learned to feel the space around me, not dodge falling rocks!"

Without another word, Fred closed his eyes and gave the stone a high toss. He reached out just at the right moment and easily caught the stone.

I was thunder struck; he made it look so easy. "But how could you know where the stone would fall?"

"My body guided me of course. I set my intention to intercept the stone and gave complete trust to my feeling center."

I spent the next twenty minutes attempting to duplicate Fred's feat, only to completely miss the rock, except for once when it smacked into my arm. Now that the stakes were higher, I had difficulty trusting in the process and my body's ability to sense the space around me. Fred said that my mind was refusing to give up control. It still thought that it was doing the sensing. He said that after my checking-in period in the mornings, feeling my feet, centering and staying grounded while walking around, I should practice the walk to the trees and the stone toss. Eventually I should be able to do both with confidence.

For the next week I practiced every day in the morning as Fred had suggested. I took along a notepad to record my experiences and checked the notes I kept of what Fred had explained so far. I could still feel the wave-like pressure from the trees but only when I was right in front of them, almost touching them. The sound was also less distinct and fainter but I refused to get discouraged. I continued and would get so thrilled and excited by the experience that I would have to just sit and calm down before I could go on. The stone toss was another matter, very frustrating, especially after being hit on the head a few times. It hurt! I just couldn't "feel" anything above me for reasons I had yet to find.

One day it was pouring down rain and I had difficulty with even the tree sensing. I asked Fred about this and he said the time would come when even a raging storm wouldn't dislodge my focus, that eventually I would be able to control the mind's interference.

I would usually practice all morning and then go have lunch. Fred ate when he felt like it. I, on the other hand, was still used to lunch and dinner at midday and early evening. Fred's advice was to eat and sleep when the body felt like it and not to impose habits out of conditioning. By the end of the week, I found his way was more realistic, and it suited living up here. After all, I didn't have any schedules to meet.

We would sometimes stay up late into the night talking or just sit near the fire and be quiet. I would explain my progress which seemed slow to me, but Fred said just to stay the course. Results would appear when they needed to.

"Natasha said you studied esoteric yoga in Europe. What's that like?"

"Your body and mind can be like wild horses that need to be brought under control before you can advance. For many thousands of years, people have kept secret the powers that they knew, so that people without guidance wouldn't harm themselves trying to develop them."

"What kind of powers?"

"Things that you are learning. The reason you are having some difficulties is that you are bumping into your conditioning. You expect instant results. Your mind needs to slow down more. Until you can master certain techniques, you will continue to be a slave to habits and patterns."

I asked him how long it took him and he said thirty years.

"Thirty years! What about learning to carve a mask? You mean I have to know all these things before I can begin to carve?"

"Of course not, but you do have to learn and experience certain things before we can begin. But you're making progress."

"Is there a faster way to learn these things?" I asked. He didn't answer but poked around the fire with a stick. I sat quietly and thought of how impatient Fred must think I was. He spent thirty years exploring. I've been at it one week and I am already wanting results. He was right of course. Our society thrives on increasing the speed and ease at which we can have things, and experience the world around us. Everything seemed to be moving faster. It was no wonder our minds speeded up, trying to stay ahead.

"There are ways to help you to develop this ability to feel with your body faster. I will show you a special room," Fred said.

He led the way into his bedroom and to what looked like a closet door in the far corner. He opened it and turned on a light.

"This little room is completely copper shielded. The copper keeps out all electrical signals and many other influences."

Inside was a table similar to a massage table, with a small pillow and a wool blanket on it. Upon entering the small room, I immediately felt a strange sensation, as if I had entered a deep underground cave, which was completely silent. Next to the bed was a night stand with a flashlight and a set of headphones. "What are the headphones for?"

" I can either bring in music or sounds, or I can talk to the person in here through them. In here, undisturbed by any outside influences, you can begin to increase your vibratory rate. The reason you felt the trees the first time was because I had you stand right next to them, plus I gave your sensing area a little wake-up call."

I asked if it was like when he touched the back of my neck at the gallery. "Similar," he replied, "only in a different region." Fred said our vibratory signal was like dropping a small stone into a calm lake. Small ripples,vibrations, go out from the source, but soon the ripples get farther apart, and have less effect as they move from the source. Drop a very large rock into the lake and the effect is much greater, the rings of influence travel further. This is why I couldn't sense the stone I tossed into the air: My own vibratory rate was still like that of a small stone. But in his copper room, I would learn to increase my signal tenfold. I asked what I was supposed to do in the room.

"Just lie down, put on the headphones and get comfortable. Then, listen to my voice and I will guide you through the process. I will be just outside the door."

After a few minutes of relaxing, I heard Fred's voice through the headphones. "Okay, I want you to begin the breathing techniques I've shown you. After a while you will begin to hear some sounds. Just stay with your breathing and continue to relax."

I became very relaxed, more than I usually did when I did the breathing techniques. The room was completely dark and silent. The space around me seemed to expand. I became aware of a slow pulsating sound that faded in and out: a metallic sound. Fred's voice became audible and he said to focus my attention on the spot where he touched me at the clearing. Once again my focus was totally centered on that place. Just as quickly, the sound now seemed to be coming from that very location. After what seemed like a long time I heard Fred's voice once again.

"Visualize the sound you hear spreading out in all directions. Do this now."

I did as he instructed and began to sense movement, as if I were moving out with the sound. I could sense a change in location. I felt like I was the sound. Each time the sound would pulsate, I traveled out further. I started to travel even farther out. Suddenly I freaked out! A voice in my head said, "Wait a minute, what's happening?"

Instantly, I was back and the sound was now just slowly pulsating.

Fred came back into the room.

"You did just fine. Take off the headphones and relax," Fred said, as I calmed down.

"That was something else. I started to move, travel out with that sound. It almost felt as if I were the sound. What was that?" I asked excitedly.

"That sound, David, was you, it was your very own energy vibration that is always broadcasting. This is the very first time in your life that you have been in a space where all outside influences ceased to distract you. It is a great advantage that you should make good use of."

"You're kidding! That was me? I mean, why did I have such fear then?"

"There are all kinds of new and perhaps strange things about your body you have never experienced consciously. This journey is not for the timid. It takes courage to explore. But there is really nothing to worry about. We have a built in protection mechanism that brings us instantly back if the ride feels threatening."

"Where would I have gone if I kept with it?"

"You're still a small stone splashing in the great cosmos—not far."

Fred advised me to use the room for a few days and trust the process. He said I should set my intentions to proceed slowly at the start of each session. He also suggested that I try to feel the ceiling in the room by projecting my energy field. "Go slowly and experiment. Enjoy this new dimension," he added.

We went back out and Fred said it was time that I was introduced to the tools I would be using to carve with. We headed over to his studio.

I was excited. Finally I might actually learn to carve. For a while I was thinking I might use up my entire time here without actually learning to carve. Also I was starting to realize that the person who stepped off the ferry was changing, into whom, I wasn't sure.

Fred brought out carving tools, a block of wet cedar and a marking pen. "These are the main tools you will use to carve your mask. I will now demonstrate their use."

The first tool he called the adze, which is used for taking off large pieces of wood. He drew a straight line near the edge of the wood with the pen, and with a short chopping motion easily took off chunks of red cedar. He kept the wood wet, which made the wood removal much easier.

"It's not so much how fast or hard you strike the wood. It's more in the way you let it fall and follow through. The wood and the adze will guide you."

He demonstrated the movement using the adze a few more times, leaving an exposed edge next to the line he drew. Next he demonstrated the crooked knife, which was used to remove finer and more precise pieces of wood. He took long, thin slivers off to show the knife's fine cutting abilities. I was totally captivated by his smooth and graceful movements. It seemed no motion was wasted. His concentration was total.

"Thank you for doing nice work," Fred muttered under his breath.

"Fred, who are you talking to?"

Fred gave me a sideward glance. "You will learn to appreciate everything around you, especially tools that do the job you expect."

"Oh, you were thanking your crooked knife," I said, knowing that he was dead serious. He said that the atoms holding the form of a crooked knife together also respond to our thoughts just as much as a crow, except the crow has many more possibilities to react. I let it go at that and changed the subject.

"So do you want me to give it a try?" I asked. He said I could practice on a discarded piece of wood, but not until I made more progress with my lessons could I begin the real thing.

"You're far from ready. Perhaps when you can catch that falling stone we will reevaluate your abilities. For now practice a little with the tools and then just hang out with them. Begin a relationship with them."

"Relationship?"

"Yes, take them to your room, and each night

spend some time holding them and talking to them."

"But Fred, what do I say? I would feel silly."

What happened next sent a chill down my spine! Fred carefully laid the crooked knife down and then held his hand over it, maybe a foot away. In an instant the knife rose straight up and the wooden handle met his open palm, which grabbed it. I didn't say anything. I was in disbelief, transfixed by what happened.

"Forming a relationship with things around you is important," Fred continued. "When you talk to your tools, speak from your heart and use kind words. They will respond back kindly."

Fred rolled the two tools up in a clean cloth and gave them to me.

"Are you going to tell me how you did that?" I asked.

"Like I said when you first got here, this is where the impossible becomes possible. You have much to learn."

✳CHAPTER FIVE

The next week flew by. Armed with new techniques I made some breakthrough advances. I paid a visit to the copper room every day, exploring further outside myself with my 'energy stream,' as Fred called it.

He was right. Anytime I felt fearful I would be back in my body in an instant. He said at this stage of my development, I didn't really travel out of my body, but rather I extended my ability to feel beyond myself. To me, it felt like I was moving out of and away from myself. The time in the room really paid off, because by week's end I had my first sense of the stone high above me in the air. I had to be well anchored in my feeling spot before I could throw the stone up into the air, otherwise my mind would interfere. I still hadn't caught it, but I could "feel" it coming down, and twice I knew where to reach for it. I just couldn't close my hand quick enough.

I didn't see a lot of Fred at this time. He was either in his room or out in nature. It seemed he left it up to me to apply what he showed me until I got results.

"Where do you go, Fred, when you're out and about?" I asked him one night as we were sitting around the fire.

"I am no different from you," Fred explained. "I practice and experiment whenever I can, although what I practice is different. There are special places near here where the energy is quite good."

" What sort of things do you practice, Fred, if I may ask?"

Fred put another log on. Then he sat cross-legged in front of the fire. "I like to check in with the animals and practice sensing what they know. Have you heard the term 'shape-shifting'?" he asked.

"Yes, that's what Natasha said crows can do. Do you believe it's possible?"

"It's a way to feel what an animal feels and to see what they see. You don't become the animal, you just transfer your awareness onto them, sort of hitchhiking and taking a ride."

As I thought about what he said. I wondered if he had hitchhiked a ride with the two crows. Fred's ability to read my thoughts now seemed commonplace.

"My two feathered friends are easy to travel with. You were some sight lying on your back after you tripped."

"So you were there? You could really see what they saw?"

"Some day you'll see for yourself. But for now stay focused on the simple things."

Simple things, as he called them had taken me the better part of two full weeks to experience, and not *fully* experience at that. And to think I could have decided not to be a student of his.

"How is conversation with your tools going?" he asked.

"Every night I tell them that some day we will carve a mask together. I am still waiting for a reply," I answered, laughing.

Fred seemed amused. "Their reply will be in the work."

I stared into the fire and thought about Natasha. I felt a desire to visit town and see her. I wondered if Fred knew my thoughts about how much I would love seeing her.

"Fred, I am thinking of going to town soon and picking up some supplies and doing laundry."

"While you're there say hi to Natasha for me, and tell her she is due for a visit."

"Apparently Fred, you can pick up on my thoughts whenever you wish. I was just thinking of Natasha."

"Guess you had better be careful what you're thinking," he replied with a wide smile.

I got up early and was in town by 8:00 am. I went to the "Raven's Nest" cafe and was told that Natasha had the day off. I stayed and had breakfast.

"Good morning David. How's it going out at Fred's?" Helen asked, pouring me a cup of coffee.

"Just great. How have you been, Helen?"

"Same as the first time I saw you, enjoying every minute I am alive," she answered, putting the coffee pot down on the table. "You know Natasha was hoping you would show up soon. I think she's sweet on you," she whispered, learning over the table.

"Really? I hope you're right, I think she's pretty special. What else did she say?"

"Oh, small talk mostly, but a woman knows when another woman is in love," Helen replied with a wide grin.

"Love! Hey, we just met."

"David, I do believe you're blushing." she said, walking away, "I'll be back. Oh, here is a Seattle paper you might want to read. Someone left it," she added, setting the paper down on the table.

It was strange glancing through the news. It seemed a world apart from what I had been experiencing with Fred. I wondered how my friend John was. As I read I became aware of the distinct feeling that someone was watching me. I looked over toward the counter and met eyes with an old man who quickly looked away. He was sort of hunched over and shabbily dressed. When Helen came back I asked her who the man was.

Helen's expression quickly turned sober. "You don't want to know, not now anyway. Let's just say some people in town are suspicious of strangers, especially if they think they hang out with Fred."

"What has that got to do with it?" I asked, glancing back at the man.

"They just don't know what Fred is up to and they stick their noses where they shouldn't be. My advice is to keep a low profile while in town and don't talk about being a student of Fred's."

I thanked her for the advice. I finished my breakfast and was about to get up, when the man from the counter started to walk past me, then stopped a few feet away. He had a wild look in his eyes.

"If you know what's good for you, you'll go back where you came from. You're doing the Devil's work, and it won't stop till Fred and his kind leave," he said, pointing a shaky finger at me.

Before I could say anything, Helen came up suddenly. "Jeb," she snapped, "if you ever want to come back in here, you'd better watch your mouth. Now get out."

The old man muttered something, turned, and staggered out the door.

"Sorry David, he usually can behave himself, but we are isolated up here. When folks get too isolated, they drink too easily, and when the Indians up here drink, it can make them crazy too—as crazy as any white man."

"That's too bad. What tribe is he from?"

"Kwakiutl. He used to be a lot more stable. Times are rough for a lot of people up here. As I said, we're pretty isolated." Helen took a quick glance around the cafe and then sat down. "Let me explain a few things for you, David."

Helen said that when Fred first came here and moved outside of town, people didn't think much about it. Eventually word got out that he was a master carver who sold his work in Seattle. The people who paid the most attention to this were a few of the local Indian carvers. They upheld a long tradition of mask carving. One of those traditions was that women did not carve. It was a man's trade, and a lot of superstition surrounded this. When the story went around that Natasha was learning to carve from Fred, some of the old carvers turned against him. They thought he had crossed the line.

"You know, Natasha told me some things about Fred, but she never mentioned the taboo part about learning to carve."

"There is a lot she probably didn't mention, but I am not the one to fill you in." Helen must have read my expression. "Oh don't worry, you just stick to your lessons with Fred and don't bother what others think. It's none of their business anyway. Well, well, would you look who's here?"

I turned and saw Natasha walking over to us.

"I knew my intuition was working right. I just had that feeling you were in town," she said, sitting down.

"You two visit, I have work to do," Helen said.
I leaned over and gave Natasha a hug, then kissed her on the cheek. "It's great to see you! I missed you."

"I missed you too, but I knew you wouldn't be bored at Fred's. How is it going?"

"I haven't started carving yet, but Natasha, I've experienced some incredible things. I really feel like I am becoming a different person. Fred is such a magical person. Oh, and he told me to tell you to come visit."

"Boy, wish I could, maybe at the end of next week. I hate to just go there for a day. I am so busy trying to save money for the winter. This town is dead in the winter with all the tourists gone. But he is right. I have to touch base with him, and you too of course.

"Hey, what timing. You have the day off, right?" I asked excitedly. She thought for a second, scanning her mental list of things to do.

"You know, I just might be able to fit you in!" she answered smiling. We agreed to meet later that day. I still had to complete my checklist, and she needed to run some errands.

After catching up on my laundry, I decided to spend the rest of the time taking pictures in town and at the seashore. The day was overcast, but there was a slight breeze. Near the shore it was chilly, but at least no harsh light. It was good for pictures. Since my arrival at Bella Namu I hadn't been in the mood to take pictures, which was unusual for me. My interest in photography had been eclipsed by Fred's lessons and the need to keep my focus on them. But now, taking pictures of fishing boats and landscapes, I realized how much I missed the experience. I saw two old rowboats hauled up high on the beach, and began taking close-ups of the many layers of brightly colored chipped paint. Inside one was an old rope curled neatly into a spiral, I used my wide-angle lens to capture the foreground rope and the beach behind. I got so involved in the scene, I didn't notice the person approaching.

"Here, take a picture of me." I turned and was surprised to see Natasha. She looked sporty in a dark blue sweater, faded jeans and boots. Her long black hair was tied back in a ponytail.

We took up residence on the beach, sitting with our backs up against a big log. Small waves broke lazily onto the shore, while large white seagulls formed a noisy horde behind an incoming fishing boat. We sat holding hands, Natasha leaning on my shoulder. Even though I was excited staying at Fred's and experiencing so many incredible new things, my heart was full of joy sitting here with her.

"What would you say if I told you I think I am in love with you?" I asked.

"I would say you had better keep your focus on what you're learning from Fred. That being said, I have to say I feel love for you too," she replied, giving me a quick kiss on my check. "So you don't have a girlfriend back in Seattle?"

I told her that my last serious affair had ended two years ago, "I really haven't been looking. And you?"

"I'm too picky. Besides, who would I find living way up here? I think I am too serious—it's Fred's fault. He hasn't been with a woman in ten years. At least that's what he told me."

"You're kidding. That's a long time. Fred is very different though. Maybe women are too much of a distraction."

"Distraction! What's that supposed to mean?"

"Well, you know, I just meant his life is so focused on discovering new things that it doesn't leave much time for a relationship."

"David, first of all you don't know Fred that well, and second, the right woman could be an asset."

Her sudden reaction had me confused. I didn't know if she was getting upset or just had strong feelings on the subject.

"You're right, I don't know Fred all that well, and some women do support a man's work."

Natasha straightened up and retied her boots. She just looked down the beach with folded arms. I got the distinct impression she was mad.

"Did I say something wrong?" I asked.

She undid her ponytail and shook her head, tossing her hair around, and then retied it.

"Let me just say something. Women don't have to support men. That is old thinking. A woman can be strong by herself. I can't believe you still think a woman is put here just as a support for a man!"

I didn't let her finish. "That's not what I meant. I was just saying that in Fred's case, she would have to be his equal in order for it to work."

What I said didn't come out right, I was defensive and lost track of the point I was going to make. Whatever the point was, it was now driving a wedge between us. Natasha got to her feet.

"David, I like you. I care for you very much, but maybe we're both too busy right now. I think we need more time. We hardly know each other."

I stood up and hugged her, but I could feel a distance had come between us. Her touch was polite but not confirming. "I am sorry if I said the wrong things. I do love you, but perhaps you are right."

We walked back to town. I told her to stay in touch, but the words sounded empty. My heart was down around my ankles as I finished up what I needed to do in town and walked to the trail that lead back to Fred's. I was in a daze; my excuse to come to town was really to see Natasha. Now it appeared my comments had caused a stir, and we parted on a sour note. I just couldn't figure out why she got so upset. I tried to make myself feel better by saying it was probably a lesson I needed to learn, that I should be keeping my attention on why I came up here in the first place.

The walk back was a sober one, not even the crows could have cheered me up.

Fred was sitting by the fire whittling on a stick when I came in. I dropped Fred's mail on the table and then walked over to make some tea.

"David, do me a favor?" he called.

"Sure, what is it?"

"Go back out and leave that dark cloud outside—the one you just brought in," he said, still whittling.

"It shows huh? I just can't figure out women!"

"What is there to figure out? They are from time, and we are from space."

"What? Now that's different."

"Make your tea, then come sit down."

Fred began to explain that because a woman's body is oriented to time, their whole world reflects that. Their bodies have monthly cycles, they are more attuned to the seasons, and their moods are synchronized to phases of the day, month and year. Their minds can remember the smallest details about when things began, even what they were doing at a particular time. In relationships, they need a lot of time to think things out and make decisions.

"You're right," I responded. "I remember many times women saying, 'I need more time.'"

"And they do. What's the rush; Time is on their side!"

"And for men, you said they are from space?"

"Yes, men's orientation is to space. They live in a world of dimensions. Space to roam, to think new ideas, to expand their work.

"That's funny. I just thought of that phrase, "I need my space."

"Yes, and it goes back to cave times when the men were out hunting, roaming, scouting for food. Space to them was everything. Women, on the other hand, knew when plants came into harvest, when to collect, the order of growing things."

"Wow, I never thought of it like that." As I sipped my tea, I thought about Natasha and how we went from closeness to distance in such a short time. "That's it. I just remembered what she had said; '*I think we need more time.*'"

I told Fred about my exchange with Natasha.

"As someone wakes up to who they really are, their true self, they begin to avoid things that sap their energy and their focus. That includes relationships. Natasha has gone far, she isn't one to waste time. If and when the time is right, she will let you know. If I were you, I would stay in your own space for now and continue on."

The way Fred said it made me laugh. He laughed

too. It was a good release to laugh. I was cheered up by the fire, and by Fred's friendship. I still didn't completely understand Natasha's outburst, how the energy between us shifted so quickly. Perhaps I'd know later, or perhaps I wouldn't, but for the moment it didn't really matter. Now it was in the past.

Before going to bed that night Fred said one last thing, "But don't forget, time and space need each other for their mutual creative expression."

*CHAPTER SIX

I woke up to sunshine and a renewed sense of energy and commitment. My stay here was an opportunity that I wanted to make the most of, and my trip into town brought this clearly into focus.

"We will be taking a hike today, so take along some water," Fred said, as he munched on some dried fruit.

I grabbed a hunk of cheese and a package of whole-wheat crackers, stuffed them into my daypack and dropped it by the front door with my camera on top. Then, I made a quick cup of coffee.

"You won't be needing the camera." Fred said.

"What if we come across something interesting?" I asked, conscious of having taken few pictures since my arrival on the island.

"If that's the case, you would be taking pictures constantly. Everything here is interesting. You will be learning a new way to see, not with a camera but with your body."

We took a trail behind the house that quickly became steep. It seemed hardly used, mostly overgrown with moss and vines, making the uphill climb difficult. It didn't seem to bother Fred though. He scampered ahead like a fit athlete. I could barely keep up, feeling out of shape. I stopped to take a rest and took a drink of water. Fred walked back. "Wait till we get to the steep part!"

"What! You've got to be kidding. I don't know why I'm so winded. You're not even breathing hard."

"That's because I am breathing right. Focus on your breath and get out of your head. You're telling yourself how steep and difficult this is. Stay inside and find your rhythm."

We took off again and I tried to keep my attention on my breathing. It helped. We hiked on until the path crested the top of a small ridge where the view was breathtaking. We had a clear sight of the surrounding mountain range that stretched far into the distance. A row of puffy white clouds moved slowly across the vista. Fred pointed to a clearing in the distance and said we would head there. Off we went, descending the trail toward the spot. I felt relief going downhill. Before long the trail leveled out and we walked at a steady pace.

We reached the place Fred had indicated and sat down. It was a grassy knoll that had a view of large trees directly in front of us, a few hundred yards ahead. We were still high enough that we could just see over the tops of them.

"Have you heard the term 'averted vision'?" Fred asked.

"Isn't that the same as peripheral vision?"

"Yes, but you can take that phenomenon a step

further. Look at those trees with your peripheral vision and tell me what you notice."

I looked just to the side of the tall trees but didn't notice anything unusual. "What am I supposed to notice?"

"Look from your 'seeing area,' as I've shown you. First close your eyes and get a fix on the spot inside and then try again."

After a few moments to tune into the area I used to sense things, I again gazed just to the side of the trees. This time I started to see out of the corner of my eyes a glow emanating from the trees. The radiance seemed to reach out many feet from the tree. I had felt it before, but this time I could actually see the glow I only felt before.

"This is truly amazing, Fred. I can actually see and feel some sort of energy coming out from the trees."

"Of course. It's their energy field. All things in nature have it in varying degrees. Look around in the same way and you will see."

I tried the same technique with other trees and even bushes that were around us. It didn't work this time.

"Your excitement has put you back into your head," Fred explained, "Reestablish your contact with the spot inside and try again."

He was right. After going inside again and reconnecting with my "seeing area," I saw the energy emitted from many more sources. The glow, shape, size and even the color was different as I gazed. Some bushes and shrubs near us seemed to change their energy's intensity as I observed. I was totally in awe. Why hadn't I ever noticed this before? It seemed so simple.

Fred pointed out a particular tree that was near us and said to pay close attention. I was to tell him when I could clearly see its energy. I centered myself and, feeling the place inside, gazed at the tree. Soon I was seeing its energy field spreading out from its branches and needles. I told him I now could see the energy clearly. He said to hold that view. "Now I want you to think of chopping that tree down with an ax."

"What!"

"Go ahead, don't hesitate."

I thought of swinging an ax into the trunk of the tree, of pieces of wood flying off. Almost instantly the tree's energy field shrunk back and turned dark. The effect was so sudden that I felt bad for the tree.

I looked over at Fred and he just gave me a nod. He knew what had just happened. "The tree picked up on my thoughts didn't it?" I asked.

"We are connected in ways you can only imagine," he replied. "Now you had better send positive thoughts to that tree," Fred suggested.

I tried the same thing again, only this time I thought loving thoughts, how beautiful the tree was, wishing it a long, strong life. Just as quickly, a broader, lighter aura spread out from the tree.

"Now you know that all around you things are responding to your presence and your thoughts. You can't hide your intent. This is why I asked you to talk to your carving tools. It wasn't just a foolish exercise."

I began to understand Fred's broader view of the

world around me. If I am constantly influencing nature around me, then I had to be clear in my intentions. I told Fred that I had heard that animals know when a hunter is in the field with a weapon and when another person is just there with a camera.

"Why do you think they disappear during hunting season? The woods speak loudly of the hunter's intentions, as does everything all around you."

We sat quietly for a while as I practiced this new technique. "If what you're saying is true, then our thoughts affect the reality that we experience, right?" I asked Fred.

"The effect we have on everything starts at the quantum level. The instant we have a thought we are changing the world around us, but it is a very small change unless we have clear and sustained intentions."

It was difficult to believe I could affect the world around me just by thinking, but then again, I was discovering that I knew very little about a lot of things.

Then, out of the blue, a lone raven landed on a high branch in one of the tallest trees. I tried to see its energy field, but couldn't. Perhaps it was too far away. I asked Fred if he thought the raven could pick up on our thoughts from such a distance.

"Animals work within morphic fields. Whatever passes in their field they can detect. The field's size varies with the species," Fred explained, sweeping his arms out to demonstrate a large area.

"So, they can't receive our thoughts unless we are close?"

"Thoughts have no space limit, but our own energy field does. That raven over there can feel our thoughts but to him it's a jumble of meaningless static. We have to focus and direct specific thoughts to get its attention. Most people's energy field is very limited because they are in their false self, the ego. If they were in their true self, their field would be immense."

I asked Fred what is our ego anyway, and how do we know if we are in it or not? He said most people believe in a separate and independent self, one that is very concrete. This "I" separates us from nature. It puts a barrier between us and everything else in the world. More importantly, it keeps us from experiencing our inner truth and energy, the very thing that would make our lives magical, full of wonder and knowledge.

"How then," he asked, "could we hope to communicate with the vastness out here? We sat in silence for what seemed like a long time. Finally Fred said it was time we continued our hike.

We proceeded on the path, passing giant cedars and hemlocks. A strong breeze began to blow the branches around, and showers of leaves and pine needles were falling along our route. I felt a new vigor and strength as we walked at a brisk pace.

We continued for another hour before Fred stopped and motioned me to be quiet. He seemed to be listening keenly to something up ahead. He sniffed the air, his head held high. He told me to wait, to remain where I was. Then he moved ahead silently. I watched as he halted further up the path. Then he turned, and disappeared into the thickets.

I waited for what seemed like a long time and finally decided to find out where he went. When I got to the spot where he left the path, I followed his steps into the thicket, but was stopped by a wide patch of blackberries. I found a small opening between the bushes and, carefully avoiding the thorns, I moved ahead slowly.

It wasn't long before I heard Fred's voice. I couldn't make out the words, they sounded foreign. Just as I peered through the bushes into a clearing, a sight froze me fast in my tracks. Fred was standing not twenty feet away from a very large bear and muttering some kind of gibberish. The large, cinnamon-colored bear was standing up on its hind legs, seemingly listening to Fred's unintelligible speech. Its huge head swayed slowly from side to side. I was so shocked that I dared not move or make a sound. Then the bear dropped down on all fours, turned and ambled off. I was still speechless when Fred turned toward me, smiling to himself.

"Didn't I say to stay put?" he finally asked.

"I didn't know where you went! You could have been attacked."

Fred let out with a belly laugh, "The look on your face! It was a good thing he wasn't hungry, you would have been easy pickings," he said, continuing to chuckle.

"Me! You're the one who could have been chomped. You were so close he would have been on you in a second!" I protested.

After Fred stopped being amused, he said that the bear was already full with berries and that his little talk had calmed it down.

"What little talk was that? I just heard a lot of gibberish," I said, glancing around, still nervous from the encounter.

"Did you see him up ahead on the path?" I asked.

"If you weren't so busy daydreaming you would have smelled and heard him too. The wind was coming straight at us," Fred said as he began picking ripe berries. I joined him and pretty soon we had two handfuls each. We sat down and gobbled them up quickly. He finally explained that what he was speaking he referred to as jibbets.

"Jibbets? Is that a language?"

"Yes, mine. It originates from a feel-good center in our bodies. Babies feel it all the time. It changes our energy field to a non-threatening and peaceful vibe. The words that spring from that place have no meaning other than a carrier for that good energy."

"You're saying that bear felt you weren't a threat because of that?"

"Of course. As long as you stay in that place it has no reason to charge you. After its curiosity is satisfied it will go about its business," Fred replied, stuffing the last of his berries into his mouth.

"Fred, is there anything you don't know?"

"Too much! That's why I am a student just like yourself."

"Yeah, right. I feel like I don't know anything. I probably would have walked right into that bear and no amount of jibbets would have saved me."

After harvesting more berries and putting them

into a bag, we continued up the trail. The wind kept blowing and it turned cold, signaling a change in the weather. I hollered up ahead and asked where we were headed now.

Fred just continued to push on without pause. I stopped to zip up my light jacket and retie my boots. I had to hurry to catch Fred who seemed hell bent on getting somewhere. I still thought about the bear who might be up ahead. I found myself getting annoyed with his relentless fast pace. I glanced at my watch. We hadn't stopped for over an hour. I was getting hungry and the one bottle of water I brought was almost gone. I made an effort to get up beside him. "Let's stop for a moment," I said, trying not to sound upset.

He examined me with probing eyes. "Is there something wrong?"

"Just a tad," I snapped. "We're about out of water, I'm hungry, and it might get dark before we get back! Where are we headed anyway?"

He stared fixedly at me without a word. Then a faint smiled appeared. "David, do you find yourself unprepared for the unknown?"

"What's that supposed to mean?" I replied, my annoyance growing. If this were some kind of test, I wasn't in the mood.

"Drop out of your head and into your body. Use what you have learned. Learn to adapt. Everything you need is all around you and within you. Stay with each breath and your frustration will leave you," he said and turned to continue on.

I swallowed hard and took his advice grudgingly, sinking into the rhythm of my breathing. I tried to ignore my mind's angry thoughts, and be positive. Finally I thought that if he could do this, then so could I. After all, I was much younger. Another hour went by and finally Fred stopped. Now the light was fading fast, and it was very cold. A heavy mist had moved in, and my concerns were back. Then I remembered the berries and reached into my pack for them.

"Not yet, we have to add a few things." Fred said.

I got the impression we were going to stay out here, long after dark with no flashlights.

"Fred, what's your plan?" I asked, holding back my mounting anxiety.

"Plan? Well, let's see, I am getting a little hungry and so I am going to find some food. It's getting a little chilly so after I eat I think I will build a fire."

I didn't let him finish. "Okay, let's get to it. Did you bring me out here to see how far I would go until I complained, because if you did, I'm complaining now! How are we supposed to stay warm, dry and fed out here in the middle of the forest, not to mention a hungry bear or two discovering us for supper!"

Fred gave me an incredulous look. "Sit down," he said forcefully. "First of all, I came up here to keep sharp the knowledge I've gained. I brought you along because you might gain a little knowledge yourself. If you'd rather rejoin the masses who are slaves to their conditioning, then go do it. Out here you can't fall victim to the laziness of the mind. Nature deals with a straight deck.

Secondly, if you can't feel comfortable exploring out here, you certainly won't feel comfortable exploring out of your body."

His scolding tone put me on the defensive, but I knew he was right. My stomach was in a knot. I wanted some kind of satisfaction, anything to appear strong. It was no use. I felt weak and vulnerable, exposed. I was tired, and my mind started working against me: *You're not cut out for this stuff. You should have stayed put in Seattle. What are you looking for anyway?*

I snapped out of it when Fred casually said, "Okay, here is the plan."

I looked up. He was now smiling and cheerful looking. I wondered how he could change his demeanor so quickly. Finally I surrendered to the situation and listened as he instructed me to search at the base of trees and underneath shrubs for any dry materials and bring them back. He would be collecting some plants and we needed to move quickly. He asked for my water bottle, saying a small stream was nearby.

I found a lot of dry grasses and weedy things along with small twigs and branches. Fred returned carrying a big pile of green leafy material. When he put them down I also saw mushrooms and four big banana slugs.

I pointed to the slugs, "You don't---"

"It's all in how you cook them!" he answered, chuckling to himself.

Fred said we would move our gatherings to a rock outcropping nearby. The face of the rocks was maybe four feet high, which he said would be perfect for reflecting back the heat from our fire. We stacked the gathered wood and the materials we had collected. Next, I helped Fred lay dead branches across a downed log to form a shelter. Inside we piled as much soft material as we could find: pine boughs, grasses and leaves. Finally we added foliage and more debris on top, until it looked like a beaver had built it. By the time Fred lit a match to the pine-pitch-covered tinder bundle at the base of the rock wall it was completely dark. Flames soon rose to the new sticks we added, and before long, we had a warm and steady fire. My spirits picked up as I heated my cold hands over fire.

Fred circled the fire with stones, and then we waited till it burned down, leaving red-hot coals. After laying small green saplings over the coals, Fred started cooking the mushrooms and slugs, which oozed out a slimy substance. I thought he was kidding about eating them but apparently he wasn't. While that was cooking, he took the berries and wrapped them in some big leafy greens. We ate these while Fred turned the food on our makeshift grill. When they were cooked, he took out a pocketknife and cut everything into small pieces.

"Try some, they are quite delicious."

I told him I would eat some mushrooms first. Fred took a few mouths full and insisted I get over my prejudice. Without further hesitation I took two fingers full and munched down, trying my hardest to think I was eating a gourmet treat. To my utter surprise the mixture was tasty and not at all repulsive. It tasted like mushrooms with a strange pleasing texture.

"Surprising, isn't it?" Fred commented. I just nodded and continued to eat. I was hungry.

The wind had stopped and fog was slowly creeping through the trees. An owl hooted at regular intervals. Fred built up the fire and afterward we watched as it danced and flickered, creating dark shadows that moved about on the rock face. Sparks popped and rose skyward into the cold night.

"I guess I acted rather foolish earlier," I said, poking at the fire with a long stick.

"We all act without thinking it through sometimes. No harm. Approach difficulties as opportunities and let your intuition guide you. Tonight you will have another opportunity. When was the last time you slept in a brush shelter?"

"Come to think of it, never," I answered, "but you seem to have no problem taking care of yourself out here. I want to learn to adapt also."

"Nature is a willing teacher if you stay centered and just learn to listen to what is being said."

Fred was right about getting another opportunity: sleeping on a bed of pine boughs and debris was anything but comfortable. It was one cold and bone aching night but I finally managed to fall asleep out of sheer exhaustion. Fred seemed to sleep soundly, remaining like a mouse curled up cozy in a bed of straw throughout the night.

Upon crawling out in the morning I was hit with a blast of cold air, and I realized then how protected we were inside the shelter. We took apart our home for the night and scattered our handiwork, then we did the same with our fire pit, digging a shallow hole to put the ashes in. Soon we were moving down the trail towards home. I had learned two valuable lessons on our hike: one, trust that Fred knows what he is doing and two, do not panic or succumb to the paralysis of the mind.

✳CHAPTER SEVEN

"Are you ready to begin carving?" Fred asked one blustery morning.

"Are you serious? You mean start a mask?" I answered, surprised and excited.

"Now is the time to apply the things that you've learned from our energy work."

I wasted no time in collecting my tools and we headed over to the studio. The rain was falling hard, coming down at a sharp angle, driven by a strong wind. I was glad he didn't suggest we go for a hike! Once inside, we hung up our dripping jackets and built a fire. Soon the room was cozy and warm.

"First I want you to do some meditation and then to visualize the face you will sketch for your mask."

I did as he requested, but after a half hour I still couldn't "see" a new face to sketch. I kept seeing an image of the mask I had held; only this time it was just a memory in my mind. I told Fred that I was having difficulty imagining anything different.

"Why don't you go back to the "copper room" and try there. I'll wait. There's no hurry."

I grabbed my coat and dashed back over to the

main house. Soon I was lying comfortably on the bed and settled into the now familiar space. I tried a technique Fred had shown me, in which I asked my subconscious to show me something. In this case it was a face to draw. While broadcasting my request, I followed my breath in and down my spine. Then, on releasing it, I visualized myself going with it, higher and higher into the sky. As usual, I became very relaxed and noticed that I no longer felt my body—I was just the breath coming and going.

Before long I felt like I was moving upward. I kept willing the unconscious to show me an image. I was startled when from out of the darkness a round-ish gray object appeared. I remained focused and alert and soon the object became a face, not yet in color, just dark and light areas. The eyes were round and saucer like, the mouth partly open with thin lips. The nose was wide and prominent with large nostrils. The face had a high forehead with heavy eyebrows. The expression was one of surprise or perhaps awe. As quickly as it appeared it went away, and I was back feeling my body.

With the face still fresh in my mind I ran back to the studio. Fred told me to sketch it before the memory faded. He brought over a moist piece of cedar and put it on the table in front of me, wiping it down with a rag.

"Now I want you to draw your design the best you can."

I took my time and penciled in the details that I recalled. When I finished, it actually looked just like the face I had seen. Fred said that I could redraw it as I proceeded.

Although I had practiced a little with the tools Fred had given me, I was nervous beginning the real thing.

"Just find your own rhythm and take your time." Fred advised.

The first tool to use was the elbow adze, which Fred quickly demonstrated once again. Soon I had chips of cedar scattered about the table, as I began reducing the large block of wood. The adze was very sharp and the wood was easy to carve. I was now on my way to completing a real Northwest Coast mask. The wind howled outside, tossing rain against the windows while I sat in the warm studio, thrilled with the work at hand.

Fred likewise worked on a mask, looking over frequently, making comments.

"Keep your fingers further back, unless you want to loose a few of them. Hold the adze at a sharper angle to the wood. You'll have better control."

I quickly learned that carving took my complete and undisturbed focus and attention. Cuts to the hand and wasted wood were the results of not being fully present. A few times my mind wondered off to Natasha, seeing her sitting here as I was, attempting her first mask. But I stopped daydreaming when a minor slip with the crooked knife nicked a finger.

"It's part of the learning process." Fred said, fetching a Band-Aid.

Part of the process was understanding how the tools did their specialized jobs. The elbow adze made quick work of reducing the wood down to take the basic shape desired. Different blade widths allowed larger or smaller pieces to be cut away. If finer pieces needed to be taken off, then the crooked knife, which was held as if gripping an ice pick, was used.

I knocked off the edges of the face, careful to leave a one-inch thick apron of wood around the bottom of the cedar. I continued to round the face and bevel the forehead. I turned the block of wood over and cut the chin in a similar way.

I had to stay aware of the developing shape to make sure that the symmetry and balance were correct, and to maintain the proper perspective. I had to redraw my guidelines many times. As I worked, my concentration led me to a state of calmness and focus so deep that all thought and action were confined only to the red cedar. Everything else receded into the background. My hearing became totally absorbed by the sounds the knife made. It was like being in a deep meditative state. Strangely though, I was aware whenever Fred came up behind me to observe my progress, he didn't distract me. If he needed to explain something or make a comment he would gently tap my shoulder first.

"Don't forget to communicate what you're doing to the wood. Mentally speak to it," he said.

Before I redrew the nose and cut in below it, I told the cedar my intentions. Next while communicating my actions, I cut the top area above the nose back to the forehead. Most of the work was done with the adze at this point. I worked slowly, stopping often to check my progress.

The quiet mood of the studio was abruptly shattered by the loud cawing of crows just outside.

"It's about time they came for a visit," Fred said, walking over to the door and letting in two wet crows. Immediately they flew over and perched up where our coats hung. They shook off the water and puffed out their feathers. Both were large with shiny jet-black coats. I was dumbfounded.

"Are these pets of yours? I've never seen crows just fly in and act like they know the place. They're not even afraid!" I blurted out.

"Pets no, friends yes," he exclaimed, "and they are smart enough to come in from the storm," he added. He retrieved a bag of peanuts from the cupboard and tossed some onto the table.

Still in awe, I watched as they flew down to the table and held the peanuts in their feet and using their sharp strong beaks like jackhammers split open the shells and took out the peanut, which they quickly ate.

"I knew they were hungry," Fred said in a casual tone.

"How long have you known them," I inquired.

"About four years now. They are still learning. Quite smart fellows!"

It was fascinating observing their actions. When they were finished with their snack they hopped around the table inspecting everything: pens, pencils, a coffee cup, everything was inspected. Fred put out his arm and muttered something, and one of them hopped up.

"Do they understand you?" I asked, becoming

more enthralled by the minute.

"Remember I said that if you focus and direct specific thoughts they will respond, especially if they trust you."

"I can see they trust you!"

Fred said that he was lucky to find their nest at just the right age and had hand fed them till they were able to fly. By then a bond was made and they would always return to roost close by each night. While they were growing up inside the studio he would repeat specific words to them whenever he fed them, words which they came to recognize. Eventually he got them to eat on cue and to hop to the table to open up small boxes that held food. Like all birds of the corvus family, they love to hide food, which they later retrieve. He experimented with all kinds of tricks and studied their behavior patterns. By his estimate they knew well over a hundred words.

"Amazing! So are you going to tell me how you "hitchhiked" a ride with them that day, shape shifting as you called it?"

Without answering Fred went over and stoked the fire, adding two more logs. After that he hung the blackened kettle over the fire, and asked if I would like some tea. The two crows flew to the top of the cedar log standing up right in the corner and proceeded to preen their feathers. Finally Fred brought over the tea and cups. We poured the tea and drank in silence. I knew Fred was mulling over my question and that he would answer in due time. He was like that.

"When you learn to travel out of your body you

will be on the other side of this dimension and in the spirit world, from which it is possible to enter other creatures and use their vehicle to explore. With my two friends here I not only could do this, but they would understand what I told them. There is no language barrier on the other side. Thought is universally understood because our higher self communicates through universal thought forms."

"But how did the crows know I would be on the trail that day?"

"I communicated to them in my out-of-the-body form. You wrote and told me when you would be coming so I was ready," he replied in a casual tone.

"So you can really travel with animals and see what they see?"

"You'll see for yourself some day if you really want to know," he answered, returning to his work.

What would it really be like to actually see through the eyes of a bird, I wondered. Fred held vast knowledge that pulled at me like a magnet. At this very moment, Seattle and my former life seemed like a distant planet. I was beginning to see that for Fred and (I suspected) many others, life was radically different from what most people could imagine. I had one foot in each world, not sure yet where I really belonged.

✳CHAPTER EIGHT

I awoke suddenly, hearing what sounded like a woman's voice. I sat up and waited but didn't hear anything, so lay back down. "Get up you sleeping bear, the day is passing you by."

This time I knew I heard a voice, and it sounded like Natasha's.

"I'll be right out. Is that you Natasha?" I hollered.

When I came out of my room, Fred and Natasha were having tea. "Natasha, it's about time you paid a visit. How are you?"

"I am great, and you?" she answered, giving me a warm embrace.

"Things have been interesting, as you might expect. I've been working on my first mask."

"Oh, I know what that is like, right Fred?" she answered, looking over at Fred who was busy sharpening some tools.

"You did just fine, Natasha, but you'd better start another before you forget how it's done," Fred replied.

We sat around and caught up on news before Fred suggested we head over to the studio.

The day was dry and warm with lots of sunshine.

It was good to see Natasha. I had forgotten all about our differences at our last meeting and I hoped she had too. Natasha came over and examined the mask I was working on.

"For someone who has never carved before you seem to learn fast. It looks great."

"With Fred looking over your shoulder how could you mess up?" I said, noticing Fred putting some things into a small backpack.

"Are you going somewhere?" I asked.

"Yes, into town for the day. You two hang out and I will see you later on."

I was totally surprised to hear Fred say hang out. It wasn't like him to suggest I neglect my lessons, and with Natasha here, I wondered why he would be going to town. I looked at her. She didn't seem surprised. She just busied herself drawing in a sketchbook. I said no more, but told Fred to have a good day in town. I was looking forward to more time with Natasha.

Fred left and I sat and worked on my mask. My concentration was faltering though with Natasha's presence. She put down her artwork and returned to my side at the workbench.

"Were you surprised that Fred went into town since you just got here? You would think he would want to visit with you," I remarked.

"Fred and I live here, but you will eventually have to go home. I am sure he knows our time together is limited," she said, draping herself over the back of my shoulders as she watched me at my work. That was too much.

I got up and hugged her. I wondered why she was so loving, when last time we were together I upset her, but I
didn't want to bring it up. Maybe I had caught her in the
wrong mood or what I said triggered some issues. At this
point I didn't care.

"Hey, why don't we go for a hike?" she suggested

I didn't even think about it. "Great! We'll make it
a picnic. We can take some food. I know a beautiful
place Fred showed me."

We gathered food, water, and extra clothes, putting them in my backpack. Before leaving I made sure my
tools were put away and the studio was clean.

It was an easy hike to the spot I had in mind. A
large open meadow greeted us, surrounded with towering hemlocks and cedars. Fred and I had been there twice
so that I could practice my averted seeing.

Normally, hiking with Fred was quiet and focused.
He rarely talked. Instead, he kept up a brisk pace as he
led the way. With Natasha all that changed. We chattered
the whole way, and stopped often to talk about the forest,
the plants, and the animal life. Natasha was a true nature
lover, and knew a lot about the area. I listened in fascination as she pointed out and described the different
properties and uses of plants.

"A complete salad exists all around us if you
know what to pick," she said, insisting that I eat some of
the leafy greens she plucked. Like Fred she knew which
mushrooms were safe to eat and showed me similar looking ones that she said could kill you.

I told her about my overnight experience with

Fred, eating edible plants, mushrooms and slugs.

She wrinkled up her nose and shook her body as if trying to shed her skin. "Slugs! You can't be serious?"

I burst out laughing just watching her reaction. "And here I thought you were a tough nature girl," I joked.

It was still a beautiful day, but with a sharp feeling of autumn around the edges. I spread out the blanket so we could sit. I could feel my desire for her rising. I had to find out if she really felt an affection and attraction to me as I did for her. "Have you ever wondered if we were meant to be together?" I asked, searching her eyes for the answer.

"I haven't told you things that I've known about us but perhaps now would be a good time," she answered, turning to face me.

She told me that Fred had told her that a certain man would come into her life, and that they would be partners. She said that when I came into the gallery she knew then I was the one he was referring to. Her life was in turmoil at the time and she really wasn't in a good place for a relationship to happen, so she kept her feelings to herself even though Fred asked her about meeting me.

"But how did Fred know that I was that person?"

"Fred can access the future. It's one of his many talents and gifts. I used to think that his ability to look into the future was totally amazing. That is, until he began teaching me how to do it. But I won't get into that now. You asked me if we were meant to be together and the answer is yes. But we have free will and can change the future. David, I really care for you. I feel love for you, you know that, but at this point in my life I'm not sure if it is the time."

I didn't let her finish but embraced her and we kissed. A surge of energy shot through my body. We held each other for a long time feeling the love that was flowing between us.

Finally she spoke. "The first time I saw you come into the gallery my pulse quickened, and I saw something familiar in your eyes. I wanted to talk with you longer, but the energy was too much, I felt off balance. That's why I left so quickly."

"I had a similar experience. I even went back out the door and thought of running after you, but instead just watched you disappear into the crowds. What was it you saw in my eyes that felt familiar?" I asked.

"Fred once said that the deeper you go into yourself, who you really are, the more you will recognize souls that share your journey, the path that you are on. I saw that in your eyes."

We kissed again and I reached under her sweater to caress her breasts. She didn't stop my advances but instead kissed me more passionately. We slipped out of our cloths and pulled the blanket over us. We were consumed with passion and everything else faded into the background. Our bodies merged, vibrating to one harmonious rhythm. We were now one being, time and space in perfect balance. Love flowed freely between us and I was overcome with joy.

We lingered in a blissful state of contentment and fulfillment.

"You know we crossed a barrier David. It will always be different now," she said.

"I know, but perhaps it was meant to be. My space now includes you. I hope the time feels right for you."

"Yes, the timing is right. I just hope this doesn't interfere with why you are here," she answered.

"But isn't this what life is all about anyway— sharing?"

"Of course, but before we can be in a place of unconditional love we have to get our false self out of the way. That is why it's important to continue to do the work that Fred has shown us. We have to respond from our original pure self; the true self."

We spent the rest of the day exploring and enjoying each other's company. By the time we got back it was getting dark. Fred had returned from town and was having a bowl of soup when we walked in.

"Fred, did you have a good time in town?" I asked, still feeling high from being with Natasha.

"I try to always have a good time. I can see that you two had a good time too," he said, glancing our way before resuming his meal.

His tone and the way he said it made me wonder what he saw in us that would indicate we were now on an intimate level. Not that it mattered, no doubt he would know soon enough.

I exchanged glances with Natasha. She just smiled and sat down at the table. Fred offered us soup so I filled two bowls, taking them over to the table. We sat in silence. The soup was hot. Before long Fred was building a fire.

I asked him how he knew Natasha and I were going to meet.

"The soul isn't trapped in the moment like our rational minds. It's more elastic, able to stretch into the past or future. On the quantum level it is boundless. Our intuition is an open channel to what the soul experiences. If you know how to really listen, you can access any information you need," he said, moving the wood around with the fire poker.

"But I have intuitive thoughts all the time. How do I know if they are from the future?"

"You have to be really conscious of them, not just responding to any feeling that comes along. You have to be ready when your intuition is channeling information, to consciously connect with it."

"Okay, how do I do that?" I asked, hoping for a direct answer that satisfied my curiosity.

"In time I will show you. For now stay put in the moment and focus on what is needed," he said dryly.

I looked at Natasha who was sitting very still and had her eyes closed. I shut up and just felt my breathing. I knew that I would frustrate myself trying to get a direct answer from Fred when he talked this way. Early on I would get impatient, wanting to have an immediate answer, but I soon learned to accept the flow of things, and understood that Fred would tell me what I needed to know when the time was right. As the fire crackled and

hissed I became very peaceful. The flames were soothing. They were the only light illuminating the three of us
sitting there.

"Isn't it strange that whenever people sit by a fire
they fall silent and just stare into it?" I commented.

"That's because it is the most ritualistic bond that
people know. When people first found fire, it transformed
their world. Fire transforms what it consumes, and as humans, we unconsciously know that we are destined to
be transformed by fire also," Fred said, adding another
log.

I thought of ancient cave-dwelling people who
needed fire for warmth, protection, and to cook their
food. That dependence must still be in our genetic code.
I asked how we are transformed by fire.

"The breath of fire is activated when we can consciously connect to it through our breathing. Then it
burns away the separateness that the ego projects,"
Natasha interjected, her face reflecting the glow from the
fire.

"People stare into fire because they are drawn into
it as if a strong magnet was tugging at their spirit. Like
Fred just said, they know on some level that this life is
one of transformation; the real self rising from the ashes
of the false self," she added.

"Wow, what a great analogy," I said.

"Closer to the real thing," Fred answered. "Just like
with physical fire we can do great harm to ourselves if
we attempt to use the breath of fire without proper guidance."

"So it's a real thing, this breath of fire?"

Fred reached over and took hold of my hand, closing his eyes as he did so. At first his hand was just warm, but quickly it became too hot to hold onto. I started to pull away but he held tightly onto my hand. I jerked my hand away frantically, certain it was burned! Both Fred and Natasha were beside themselves laughing at my reaction. When I realized that in fact my hand wasn't harmed, I just shook my head. "How did you make my hand heat up like that? Your hand felt as if it were a hot iron."

"Just giving you a practical example of the fire within. Now you know it is real," He said, holding up his palm as if to say there was no trick involved.

"When you're hot you're hot," Natasha said, as they broke out into another round of laughter.

I pointed a finger at Natasha. "You just wait till I can do that, then we will see who's laughing."

I woke up late in the morning from a deep sleep after having stayed up too late with Fred and Natasha. I had offered my room to Natasha but she insisted on using the big couch near the fire. After coffee and a light breakfast she headed back to town and promised to visit more often. I said I would try to make it to town soon. I went over to the studio where Fred was busy with his work.

"Good morning," he said, as I sat down at the workbench.

"Morning," I replied, taking the wet cloth off my carving.

"Aren't you forgetting something?" he asked.

I thought for a moment, and then realized I hadn't done my daily practice at the clearing, in fact, this was the second day without it. I was used to starting each day that way and wondered how I could have completely forgotten it.

"You're right. In fact I missed yesterday too. Guess I should head out there."

"Romance can do strange things to our psychies."

I laughed to myself and realized maybe he was right: All I thought about was Natasha. My focus had shifted slightly. I asked Fred if missing a day or two was really such a big deal.

"The momentum you have built up will slip away faster with each passing day until the forces competing for your attention will sabotage your efforts."

He went on to say that letting my mind dwell on past experiences with Natasha would also leave me out of the present moment and more importantly, distance me from my intuition.

"You mean it can happen that fast? Surely after a straight month of concentrating on my lessons I've built up some momentum."

"Where you put your focus is where you'll be. The momentum you build up with daily practice will protect you from the false self, the part in you that wants to be in control," Fred said in a stern voice.

"Your intent and focus is all you have to overcome your ego. While you sleep, it doesn't. It works overtime to devise ways to deceive you."

I thought he was being over dramatic, like this evil

thing is waiting at any moment to pounce, to find a way into my soul. It was starting to feel like an argument and I didn't want that so I just told him that he was right. Then I casually said that the energy sure changed fast in the room.

"Energy! " he said, squinting his eyes. "Energy doesn't give a hoot about you, me, or anything else for that matter, it just is. It will take the path of least resistance. If you don't shape it, focus and direct it, it will eat you alive. The same fire that helps you can destroy you."

This was the first time I really thought Fred was angry. The look he gave me was fierce and forceful. I sat still and tried to consider what he was saying but was now feeling angry and confused. While I sat stewing over his words he turned to face me. He was sitting at the other end of the bench, maybe twenty feet away and began moving his hands in a circular motion as if feeling the outside of a large ball. "Here, catch this." he said and flung an invisible something at me.

In an instant I felt a force slam into my chest, nearly knocking me off the stool. A wave of fear swept through me, gripping my hands, freezing my will, disallowing any action I might take. I found myself in a state of shock and couldn't move. Nor could I hear anything. I was suspended in a very odd place. Thoughts and sensations flooded my head, each with its own texture and color. I felt on the verge of panic. All this happened in quick succession until I finally heard Fred's voice, which had the effect of stopping the turmoil.

"Now do you know why you need to check-in?"

"I don't know what I need right now," I replied. Then I got up and lay down on the couch nearby, I was still in a pathetic state, drained of energy. When I finally felt better, I asked Fred what had just taken place, what was the force that hit me, and what about the thoughts and sensations, the crazy mind space I experienced. He pulled his stool over and explained in a calming tone that he had sent me a raw energy ball that flowed directly into my state of mind at that very moment. Since I wasn't centered and grounded it had the effect of confusion, doubt and anger. He said that this is what it's like for some people. They are a channel for too much raw energy, energy they aren't able to control.

"Each new day we have an infusion of raw energy, but in small amounts. We need to channel even those small amounts properly, otherwise it goes directly into old patterns that do nothing to create a new person." He said by doing my daily exercises I'm slowly but surely rewiring my system to handle larger amounts of energy, that I can then direct safely.

"I think I am beginning to see it clearly now," I said, with a shaky voice. "If a person isn't ready, it will be destructive, right?"

"Now you're getting it. This work is not for the weak at heart. As you gain access to greater amounts of energy, you have to be willing to accept greater responsibilities. You can't just drift back into old habits because that new energy load will burn you out."

I was feeling better, but still in awe of Fred's power. It seemed just when I was starting to get used to his ways, he unleashed another surprising ability. He could be a frighteningly powerful person; I was learning never to take him for granted.

"You're going to have to show me how you were able to toss energy across the room like that," I said, "but not at me this time!" I added, laughing.

"You should understand that what I did takes a lot of practice and control, but I can give you an idea what is involved," Fred answered, walking over to my mask on the table. "Come over here and put your hands on your carving."

I got up from the couch and sat in front of my carving. Next he instructed me to put my hands on either side of the wood, cupping it. Fred stood behind me and put his hands on my shoulders. "Now feel the energy circulate through you and the wood."

Almost at once I felt a tingling sensation that became a warm flowing sensation that ran down one arm, into my hand and into the wood. It continued up the other hand and arm and proceeded to flow around in a circular motion. The experience was very pleasant, not at all like the blast I had just received.

"This is great Fred, it's like a little electric current going traveling around in a circle."

Fred took his hands away and the flow stopped.

"I am just directing a flow of energy, no big deal, but this is the first step in directing energy. If your intentions at the time are strong and clear, then the wood will be infused with those same intentions. This is the beginning of creating a mask with power."

"So somehow the wood retains energy from us?" I asked.

"Ahhh, yes, back to intentions. It's always back to our intentions. They pretty much call our world into being, whether it is carving, speaking, making love or just daydreaming, we continually direct energy in one form or another. Most people's thoughts are a jumble of wants and desires that support their emotional addictions, which in turn supports their habits and patterns. Their world remains the same, void of the spontaneous magic which resides within each moment."

"I just had an insight—why people sometimes know who's calling right before the phone rings. They receive our intentions to call at that moment."

"Good, you're starting to understand. Now I want you to hold your hands apart like this," Fred asked, holding his palms a foot apart from each other. "Then slowly move them together and see if you can feel the energy between them."

I closed my eyes and did as he said; slowly bringing my palms toward one another. Finally they touched but I didn't detect anything. He asked me to relax and keep my focus on just the area between my hands. After a few minutes of breathing slowly and centering myself I tried again. This time I could perceive a slight pressure between my palms, as if I were compressing something. I kept trying, keeping my attention on the space between. Fred whispered to move my hands in and then out slowly. As I did this I began to feel the same pressure but with a warmth. As my hands came closer together the warmth increased, and moving them apart decreased the sensation. It now felt like a warm flow between my palms, becoming stronger and weaker as the distance between shrank or grew.

"It's working," I said, "I can feel the energy get stronger and weaker."

"From this simple example you will have something to build upon. Next you can learn to control that flow and shape it and finally direct it. The energy ball you experienced was the result of this little exercise."

✳CHAPTER NINE

A week passed while I continued to practice sensing energy between my hands as well as the other exercises Fred had shown me. It seemed I had found a new level of concentration and focus. I was now able to experience most of what Fred had demonstrated to me. It became easy to feel the energy being emitted from trees and shrubs, and how my thoughts could change those energy fields. I could sense the space above me and 'know' where the stone was falling.

I was slowly getting in touch with nature like I never believed was possible. It confirmed my belief that everything is alive and responsive to what we think and do. My sessions in the copper room clarified my visions and intentions. I was still not able to leave my body for flights out into the spirit world, but realized that I still harbored some basic fear of doing so. Fred said not to worry about it, that in time I would feel safe. I wanted to see through the eyes of animals, to feel what they felt. I doubled my efforts to get past the fear and gain control of the techniques necessary.

The basic face features of my mask were nearly complete now, and I noticed that a strong sense of connection had developed with it, almost as if I were bringing something into the world. One day, sitting at the worktable, I realized that I too was being worked on, and a new part of myself was emerging. Fred had been right when he said the students work on themselves more than the mask they are carving. In the process, I was slowly removing a mask that I'd worn all my life and was learning how to live authentically.

"We're going into town today," Fred announced. "Take a towel with you."

"A towel?" I asked.

"Yes, a towel. You know, what you use to dry off with."

I didn't ask again what he was up to, but collected a few things including the towel, and soon we were off down the trail to town. Usually Fred took the lead when we took walks, but this time he asked me to lead the way. I set a steady pace but for some reason was very conscious of Fred behind me, as if he were observing my movements.

"Are you walking within your breath?" he asked behind me.

I stopped and told him that yes—I was staying centered and keeping my attention on my breathing. I also told him that I felt he was observing me.

"Now that you're aware of yourself and me why don't you try walking with your eyes closed?"

"Are you serious? This isn't an open meadow. It's a narrow winding path that has hard trees to bump into to," I answered smiling, hoping he wasn't really asking me to try. I knew I could now sense trees and objects near me without too much effort, but that was in a large open area and walking slowly around. What he was suggesting out here was out of my league.

"Here, I brought you your blindfold," he said, tossing me the same one I used before. "Trust what you know and just move slowly. I will be right behind you."

I knew it was useless protesting. I put the blindfold on and did my best to go inward and stay with my sensing area. I ignored my mind's attempt to call a halt to this crazy experiment and went forward. At first it wasn't so bad. I could sense the trees on either side of me as I crept along. Another clue was the trail was a lot smoother than on either side of it, where it was littered with sticks and growth. At one point I walked into a bush that I didn't feel at all, and when I finally backed out of it, I was too disorientated to know where the path was. I called to Fred to give me an idea where I was.

"I am still on the path so orientate yourself with my voice."

After a few attempts I managed to walk straight for him till his outstretched hand stopped me. "Now turn around and begin again," he instructed.

"At this rate we will never reach town!" I said, laughing to myself.

"You might not, but I will."

"What's that suppose to mean?" I hollered back.

"Just keep sensing your way."

We continued on, and I started to get the hang of it, if I went slowly. Finally, Fred announced that I could take off the blindfold.

"You did well for your first go around. You never know when you might get caught out in the dark without any light and have to travel by feel alone. It's a good skill to perfect."

Fred took a detour off the trail and we ended up at a beautiful stream. It was about six feet across and I could see a few nice pools further down. We headed down to the pools. "Strip down and immerse yourself completely," Fred said, motioning toward one of the pools.

"Now I know why I had to bring a towel! This water is freezing, " I said as I knelt down and splashed some water around at the stream's edge.

"You have the knowledge to deal with it, that's what your practice is for."

I had to give myself some rational reason to do this thing, so I told him that at least I would be nice and clean if I saw Natasha in town. My jokes didn't elicit any sympathy from Fred who shook his head and quickly undressed. This was the first time I ever saw Fred bare-chested, let alone nude. I couldn't believe his body; not an ounce of fat on his trim and muscular build. If I didn't know better, I would swear his body was that of a twenty-year old.

Without hesitation and with deliberate calm he went into the icy pool, which was deep enough to come to his waist.

"Well at least you're going to join me in suffering," I quipped in a nervous tone. But he didn't hear me. He was already beneath the water, sitting motionless at the bottom. I peered into the pool and was shocked to see him completely still, holding a large rock in his lap to hold himself down. In total fascination I watched him stay in that position for what seemed minutes, before finally rising back to the surface.

"Fred, you're unbelievable! Aren't you freezing?"

He didn't answer but just pointed at the water and then me. Obviously it was my turn. I took a few quick breaths and slipped into the swirling pool. I gasped as the cold water enveloped my body. Instinctively I wrapped my arms around myself and fought to catch my breath.

"Don't fight it. Let go to the water and put your attention on your center. Do it now."

I had been in cold water before, but this felt worse. My feet and ankles were already feeling numb. Fred said to crouch down and let the water flow over me and stop fighting it.

I gathered my courage and sank deeper, letting the water run over me. My head felt like it would certainly freeze as I tried to stay focused. Within seconds I burst back out. I could hear Fred laughing.

"Damn that's cold," I insisted. "How do you stand it?"

"Concentrate on heat spreading throughout your body with each breath you take in. Feel its warmth and let go of resisting. Resisting will only keep you in your head. Try again."

I was so cold by now, that it didn't really matter going under again. This time I just let go of thinking how cold I was and did as Fred suggested. Much to my surprise, I began to feel warmth spreading throughout my body. It started just above my stomach where I was told to concentrate, slowly spreading out in all directions as if a warm liquid was coursing through my veins. I sat near the stream's bank with just my head out of the water and soon I didn't feel cold at all, even though I was well aware of the frigid stream swirling around me. I felt wrapped snugly in a protective cocoon, but I noticed that if I moved too quickly the cold water would be felt again.

At one point I realized that my head sticking out of the water was the only cool spot, that my body was now comfortably warm. I made the mistake of daydreaming about seeing Natasha, and I lost my focus. Almost immediately the icy water broke through. I recoiled in defense. I tried to regain warmth but it was no use, the cold water came back with a vengeance and I leaped out shivering. As I grabbed the towel to dry off, Fred also got out. We both dressed. I told Fred my experience.

"We go where our thoughts are. Stay in your body the next time and the cold won't get to you."

"Don't tell me," I said, "you never know when you might get caught in an icy cold stream and need to stay warm." I joked with Fred.

"Many people can put up with very cold water for a long period of time, but what I wanted to show you was how to control your body's temperature. You can use the same technique if it's too hot—to cool yourself down."

"I'll have to find a nearby stream to practice this one."

"From now on try taking cold showers till you can regulate your temperature at will, then go back

I told him I would consider it. I was very much attached to hot showers at this point, especially up here where the autumn air was brisk and the days were growing colder.

Once in town, we visited the post office and then the general store where Fred ran through his checklist of items to buy. We filled up our packs with an odd assortment of things. There were strike anywhere matches, bootlaces, soap, more candles, sea salt, waterproofing wax, iodine, sandpaper; on and on until Fred had what he needed to keep on hand for the coming winter months. Our packs were full and heavy by the time we walked into the Raven's Nest to have a bite to eat.

"Well, well, look who blew into town. How are you Fred? David?" Helen said, walking up to our table.

"Just fine Helen, how are things going?" Fred replied.

"Same as same can be, except the tourists are beginning to thin out. Before long it will just be Natasha and myself taking orders from the locals. So how is your pupil, David here, doing? Is he a master carver yet?" she asked smiling.

Fred puckered up his lips and gave me a long look. "He has what it takes—courage and curiosity. Time will tell if he applies them."

Helen took our order and then I asked if Natasha was working today.

"She is off today but I imagine she will pop in

sometime. Are you going to be in town long?"

"It's up to Fred," I said, looking over at him.

He just shrugged his shoulders and said we would see. Halfway through our meal I noticed two men walk in and head for the counter. One was Jeb, the crazy Indian I had encountered before. I don't think they noticed us, but I mentioned it to Fred. He just shook his head yes, he knew.

They made me nervous and I couldn't relax and enjoy the food. I took a drink of coffee and then noticed Jeb scan the room, stopping on us. He narrowed his eyes and made some comment to the other man with him. Fred didn't appear to be alarmed in the slightest but just continued to drink his tea and make notes in the little book he carried. It wasn't long before the two men got up and walked over. Helen immediately tried to intervene, but Fred waved her off.

"So you finally came out of your hiding," Jeb sneered.

Fred just continued to drink and draw in the book.

"I am talking to you, Mr. Magic man."

The room fell silent, and I was beginning to get mad. The smell of alcohol from the two further inflamed my mounting anger. I started to express myself but Fred interrupted me, putting his hand on my arm.

"Why don't we all go outside in the back and discuss this, " Fred said, rising carefully from his seat. We walked out the back door to an open area with the two men following close behind. Once outside Fred stopped a short distance from the back door and turned around, telling me to stay on his left side. As soon as the two men came through the door my anger took over and I told them if they had something to settle they would have to deal with me first.

"Suit yourself boy," Jeb said, putting his hand inside his jacket, as if reaching for a weapon. Before they could make another move, the back door swung open and Natasha burst out.

"Dad, you promised you wouldn't make trouble!" she screamed.

I quickly glanced at Fred, "That's her father?" I gasped.

"Stay back, Natasha. This doesn't concern you." Jeb growled.

"It does concern me. You're drunk and don't know what you're doing," she pleaded.

"Stay back I said," Jeb yelled, pushing her aside.

Fred closed his eyes and held out both his palms facing the two men as they lunged forward, Jeb holding an iron pipe, his friend a piece of chain wrapped around his hand. What happened next completely stunned me.

Jeb and his partner were violently knocked off their feet by an energy that Fred projected, sending them to the ground. They attempted to get back up, but Fred again sent them sprawling to the dirt. They were now so confused and shaken they just crawled to the edge of the cafe. Natasha was backed up against the building with one hand over her mouth in disbelief.

Fred calmly walked over to the visibly shaken pair who now recoiled at his approach.

"It's not my wish to harm you, but you must leave immediately."

Without uttering a word both men scrambled to their feet and stumbled back through the door, knocking into tables as they exited through the front door.

Fred went to Natasha and embraced her. She buried her head in his chest. Helen stuck her head out the door and asked if everything was all right. Fred just gave her a nod, and said not to worry. I wanted to say something, but was at a loss for words. I suddenly felt awkward and out of place. I walked past them and went inside and sat down.

"Honey, are you okay?" Helen asked.

"Why didn't anyone tell me that Jeb was her Dad?" I asked, shaking my head.

"It wasn't my place to tell you. You and Natasha need to have a long talk. Can I get you something, a cup of coffee maybe? We have a fresh berry pie just out of the oven."

"No thanks, Helen, I think I'll just sit for a while."

My stomach was still in a knot when Fred and Natasha came in and sat down. Both were relaxed and appeared as if nothing had happened. I stared into an empty coffee cup with a head full of confusion.

"David, I am sorry I didn't tell you about my Dad. I was too ashamed. He wasn't always like that."

I looked into her eyes and my anger and confusion melted away. She was smiling, but her eyes were holding back tears. Fred too was smiling with love and compassion in his eyes. He got up and came around behind me and put his hands on my shoulders.

"You two have a talk. I am going to take care of some things in town, I will meet you a little later on."

Natasha pulled her chair closer. Helen brought over some tea and a plate of cookies.

"Just in case you need a snack," she said.

While we sipped tea, Natasha began to tell me about her father and much more.

"I grew up in a culture of highly skilled mask carvers, and my dad was one of them. I am part Indian and part French from my mother's side. She was a painter who had a studio in Vancouver. They had met there. She let him display his mask carvings at the studio-gallery, that she owned.

For a while they both lived in Vancouver. That's where I was born."

"Where is your mother now?"

"She was killed in an auto accident when I was ten. My father took me back to live here, and he tried to carry on, but never got over her death. He started drinking and lost all interest in carving, so he ended up working on fishing boats to support us. When he wasn't working he would drink and become abusive. Finally I had to move out on my own. My relationships were likewise abusive and I became disillusioned with them. Helen took me in and gave me the support that I needed. Finally I went to live with my mother's sister in Vancouver for a period of time, trying to sort my life out, eventually moving back here. By then my father was the way he is now. We mutually avoided one another, but in a small town that's not easy."

"Wow, what a tragedy."

"You know though, eventually I accepted him as he was, and tried to show love toward him but the alcohol had taken its toll. He had become someone else. You know I think I am ready to move from here for good, but I would miss Fred."

"Helen told me that when you learned to carve from Fred, the local carvers turned against him. The reason being he was teaching a woman to carve. Now I know why your father came up to me, pointing his finger, saying angry things. It makes sense that he would dislike me also." I stopped speaking for a moment, and took both her hands in mine

"Why don't you move back with me," I asked.

Natasha squeezed my hands. "I can't promise you anything at this time David. Part of me says yes, but I have to be sure it is the right thing. Really the only reason I remained here so long was Fred. He has shown me a stronger, truer part of myself."

"In a way he has brought us together. Now it is up to us to explore the reasons why," I said, kissing her cheek.

I decided to phone my friend John to check in on how things were in Seattle. Natasha and I agreed to meet later. On the way to use the phone at the post office, I ran into Fred who was chatting with someone on the street.

"David, I want you to meet a dear friend of mine," he said, as I walked up. He introduced me to a man about his height, with a dark complexion, wearing a unique looking little round hat. His clothes were also unique: a sleeveless jacket that had interesting designs stitched on it and light orange pants. Contrasting with these was a pair of white tennis shoes. "This is Dorge, recently back from Tibet."

As we shook hands, I immediately felt a strong connection with him. His smile was warm and he seemed very charming. It was his eyes and the look he gave me, that suddenly triggered some deep emotion to the point that I felt tearful. Something in his eyes entered me and remained. I looked down at the ground, suspended in my feelings for a moment.

"Fred tells me that you have been making great progress."

"He has?" I said, looking back up and over at Fred, who was now grinning.

"You don't mind if Dorge stays with us for a while do you?" Fred asked.

"Of course not, that would be great. I would love to hear about Tibet. Is that where you first met?" I asked Dorge.

"I guess you could say that. We've known each other a long time," he answered, exchanging glances with Fred.

We chatted a little longer. Then I excused myself to go make my phone call. Walking away, I noticed that my mood had changed. I was now feeling very upbeat. Something took place between us, as if a heavy weight had been lifted. I was actually feeling very happy.

After a few attempts I managed to reach John at his wood shop.

"David! Well I'll be damned. You're still alive. How are you?"

"Great John. Too many things to go into now, but everything is one big adventure here. I haven't completed a mask yet but I am getting close."

"So what the heck do you do with your time off up there—chase the local female natives?"

"Very funny, no actually I keep pretty busy with lessons Fred gives me."

"Like what?"

"Well, it all has to do with getting in touch with a bigger part of who we are. I'll explain it more when I see you, but it's things like visualizations, focus, staying centered, does any of that make sense?"

"Hey, you know me, I just work wood. I don't have time to work on myself, but it sounds interesting. What's the weather like up there? It's been gorgeous down here. When are you headed back?"

"Not sure yet, I really want to complete this mask and there is this woman up here—but that's another story I'll have to tell you."

"I knew you would run into someone, even out in the sticks. Is she beautiful?"

"I think so, but in a different way."

"What's that supposed to mean, like whether or not she has her dentures in?" he answered, chuckling over the phone.

"John, you never change. Hey, what's new in Seattle?"

"Not much, been too busy to notice, except the price of gas is skyrocketing again. I'll have to raise my prices."

We talked till I got bored hearing about the life I thought I was still part of. Listening to John showed the contrast. I was a different person now. I wondered if I could return to the same life I knew before.

I found Fred, Dorge, and Natasha at the cafe where we agreed to meet. I put down my pack and sat next to Natasha.

"Get everything taken care of?" Fred asked.

"That's it. I don't need to do anything else, except to eat something."

I told them about my conversation with John and how I felt afterwards, while Dorge and Fred sat, nodding their acknowledgment from across the table.

"You will never find the same satisfaction in things that seemed so important before," Dorge said.

"New friends will replace old ones. People who vibrate at a higher level will enter your life because you will be attracting them," added Fred.

"So, Dorge, tell me more about Tibet." Natasha said.

"If you ever get the opportunity, go. It will affirm the things you are learning here. People by nature are wiser and more in touch with their inner life there. The collective energy is uplifting, making it possible to sustain long periods of concentration and focus. I've been fortunate to have spent much of my life there."

"Are you Tibetan?" I asked.

"My father was from Nepal, but my mother was German. They met in Nepal, so I guess you could say I am a Nepalese-German," he answered, smiling.

Natasha leaned over and told me that Fred was his student at one time. "No way!" I blurted out. "I mean you don't look old enough to be his teacher," I told Dorge.

"Fred was one of my first students many years ago," he replied.

He actually looked much younger than Fred so I assumed he was probably in his forties. I nearly fell over when he said that he was past seventy!

"Age is immaterial." he said. "In the bigger picture, and in a broader reality, age is an illusion, but the body is governed by the laws of duality, meaning the struggle between our conditioned selves and our true spirit."

"But how do stay so young looking?" I asked.
"A lot has to do with proper breathing and attitude. It also helps to live intuitively instead of out of conditioning."

"Wow, I'm impressed."

"There are some side benefits to living closer to reality as you can see," Fred said, and then announced that it was time to head back. I told Natasha that I hoped she would come visit again soon, that I missed her. She voiced similar sentiments and walked with us to the start of the path where we hugged good-bye.

✳CHAPTER TEN

Dorge made himself comfortable, living in the main room of the house. He said sleeping on the couch was more than he was used to. His usual bed was no more than thick woven blankets thrown down.

In the first few days back from town, I didn't know how to approach him. I had many questions to ask, but somehow felt intimidated by his presence. He and Fred were very different. I was used to Fred's mannerisms and his way of teaching: direct, but kind and understanding. Dorge felt like I was coming up to the rim of a deep gorge at night and hearing the faint roar of the river below. It was wise to pay close attention to where you stepped, lest you fell over the edge. At night, sitting in front of the fire, I would notice him observing me, every once in a while saying to himself, *Uh-huh, Uh-huh*, like he was confirming something he saw. I wanted to ask him about it but resisted, telling myself that I would ask later. Fred for the most part sipped his tea, tended the fire and made small talk about the weather and the need to prepare for winter. On the third day everything changed. Fred said that Dorge was going to accompany me for my morning practice in the clearing.

It was drizzling and cold as we entered the clearing. I didn't know what to expect so I told Dorge that I was going to run through my daily exercises that Fred had taught me. He said fine and that he would just observe.

I did my usual walk around the clearing feeling my feet, becoming centered and grounded. Next I sat down and closed my eyes, visualizing my breath entering the top of my head, down my spine and then back up and out again. I did this until all I could feel was the energy flowing in and out. Finally, I slowly came back to feeling my body, and opened my eyes. Dorge was seated cross-legged on the ground observing me. He sat very still, completely focused and composed. He gave me a nod, and in a soft voice said, "Go on."

I closed my eyes again and concentrated on the feeling center that allowed me to experience the energy field around trees. I walked slowly toward the stand of trees directly in front of me until I started to touch their energy field, stopped, turned around, and slowly walked back. By now it was easy and I ended up where I started.

I asked Dorge if he knew what I just did and he said yes, then asked if I would like to experience nature in a fuller way. I said sure, if that was possible, what did he have in mind? He then got up and walked over to me.

"Here is all you need to do," he said, "just open your mouth wide and take in a deep breath."

I just looked at him for a moment, "That's it?" I asked. "Open my mouth and take a breath?"

The next series of moments seemed to happen all at once even though I distinctly remember each part. I heard a voice say, *"You are ready for the next step. Open your mouth and take a breath."* The voice sounded like him but was deeper and slower, like a recording played at a slower speed. Without hesitating I opened my mouth and took in a big gulp of air just as I saw his hand, with palm up, in front of my face. He made a motion like blowing something out of his hand and into my mouth just as I took in the breath. The next instant felt like someone flipped on a switch in my entire being. I could see the flow of energy moving throughout everything. It seemed as if every cell in my body was now in tune with the nature around me. I was completely in awe and rapture. A bird flew by overhead and I could feel its wings beating. I was the bird at that moment in flight. I felt a profound oneness with everything around me. Tears of recognition began running down my cheeks, but I was neither sad nor happy. Another part of me knew what this moment meant and I rejoiced in the magic of it all. I looked over at Dorge and he was just glowing with a loving spirit; kindness pouring out in all directions.

I walked around and yet wasn't even aware that my feet were touching the ground. It was more like I floated over the earth. I then realized that my body was just a container, a vehicle that housed my spirit. My mind had little or no thought; intuition was now a direct channel to knowledge and understanding.

Insights to questions long asked began to be answered. I knew that there was nowhere to go, nothing to become, everything was already perfect in the world and universe. God was everywhere in all things. The separation we felt was nothing more than a thin veil, made up of conditioning that we simply identified with. Nothing was solid. Light and energy took expression through the myriad of forms we experience and were the only things that were real.

It had stopped drizzling and the clouds parted, letting through shafts of light. At that very moment I experienced an overwhelming urge to leave, to just leave this body and move up into that light, merging back into it. I felt a hand on my shoulder and turned. Dorge looked like the most radiant being I had ever experienced. "You have things to complete here and more to learn," he said.

"Do you have any idea what I am experiencing right now? Was it something you did that allowed this?" I asked, wiping away tears.

"It's the first breakthrough that every real seeker has. You could say that it is the most conscious moment of this life. You will always refer back to it for confirmation as to what is real. For now just enjoy it and we will talk later. I will see you back at the house," he replied, squeezing my shoulder before turning and walking away.

I remained in this altered state for another hour until at last I returned to my normal self. Then my head was once again filled with thoughts, and no matter what I tried, I couldn't get back to the experience. Still, I was left in a profoundly serene and calm state of mind. I sat up against a tree and thought about everything that had taken place.

What had Dorge done when he seemed to blow into my mouth, which led to my experience? I didn't have an answer to the question, but somehow it didn't matter. I headed back to the cabin knowing a major shift had taken place in my understanding of what this life was all about. I realized that my struggles were self-induced, that life was in fact perfect in every way.

It was my ego's view that clouded that reality, that false sense of who we think we are that we believe in so deeply, while all around us and through us exists a harmonious and perfect oneness.

Fred and Dorge were sitting at the table when I entered. Fred looked up grinning from ear to ear. It was obvious he knew what had happened.

"Guess you now know that all is well," he said. "No matter what happens in your life now, you know for sure that there is a perfect place that you are a part of, a place called Perfection. The more you let go to it, the more you will be in that magical experience. It is just your not-self, your ego, that keeps you from it," Fred said.

I could feel tears forming again as he spoke.

"But why me?" I asked. "Just because I have practiced a few techniques? I am no one special."

"Lucky for you, you're not!" Dorge said, "Otherwise your ego would be telling you right now how special you are, that you must be special in some way to have had such an experience! As far as why you had that experience and not one of your friends or anyone else you know, I could say that you have prepared in a former life or I could just say your lucky number came up. But all of that isn't what's important. What is important is that you have consciously crossed a line from ignorance into bliss, now you know. Whatever else you do in this life will always have that experience as a background."

Fred went on to explain that the "death gong" to my ego had now officially sounded and it would be scheming up ways to distract me. "It knows its control will eventually come to an end," Fred said.

I told him that carving a mask didn't seem important at all anymore.

"On the contrary, you now understand that our actions allow the flow of that spirit, that energy, to touch whatever we engage in. It is all about creating: to inform, to heal or to share. What you do now can be infused with a part of you. Life is one blissful, creative moment with each breath."

Dorge excused himself, saying that he was going to use the copper room. Fred brewed a pot of tea and I found out more about his teacher.

They met in Tibet over thirty years ago when Fred was visiting. At the time Dorge was working with the local children, taking the advanced ones aside and giving them techniques to practice. Fred recognized him immediately as his teacher, and stayed in Tibet for four years studying with him.

"What did you study?" I asked.

"Things that one day you will learn if you continue along this path."

I asked if he knew Dorge was going to give me the experience I had.

"Of course. That's one reason he is here. He is part of your tribe"

"Tribe?"

"Each of us is part of a soul group, attracted to one another by vibration. Souls from many dimensions can participate at the same time and in the same place. Whether we are conscious of it or not, we are helping one another toward self realization so that eventually we can all be a soul group that is ready to move into greater forms of service to the whole."

"Perhaps that's why I felt a strong connection to him when we met. Are you part of the same soul group?"

"Yes and so is Natasha."

"What do you mean by many dimensions at the same time? Do we learn on different levels?"

"We are so used to thinking in a linear way, that it is difficult to grasp the idea of being in two places at once and having many different experiences simultaneously, but that's exactly what we often do in dreams."

"I remember feeling very odd in dreams, like I was in some other dimension and experiencing someone else. Is that what you mean?" I asked.

"You're close. In dreams we are using only a small part of our awareness so things don't have continuity. As we become more aware, our dream world begins to make more sense. Then we can advance even in our dreams."

Fred said that was what Dorge was doing right now, checking in with his teachers on the other side.

"You mean out of his body?"

"Yes, he can meet with beings of his soul group and transfer knowledge back and forth quickly, even in other dimensions.

"When we experience life from only one perspective, our lives become very personal. We then consider our own motives and no one else. We can spend our whole lives believing that we are alone; therefore we work hard at developing and keeping control. If we can let go of wanting control and begin to trust in a greater reality, we can move forward faster."

I began to feel very sleepy and tired and told Fred I was going to lie down for a while. He said it was very natural to feel drained after experiencing such a high level of energy that I wasn't used to. I went to my room and immediately fell into a deep sleep.

I woke up suddenly and for a brief moment didn't know where I was. I felt totally disorientated. It was dark outside; I wondered how long I had slept. Finally, as things appeared normal again, I remembered my dream. I was out on a great plain, a vast expanse of desert-like land. I was just scanning the area as if my vision could telescope in and out to inspect any part of it. I spotted a lone figure in the distance and immediately I crossed that distance and was standing in front of him. It was Dorge. He reached out and put his hand on my shoulder, then pointed toward a group of beings coming toward us. As they approached I intuitively knew that they were part of my soul group. As I looked at each being, each one telepathically conveyed information and images to me as he or she came closer. It seemed perfectly natural to "know" about their experiences on other worlds besides earth. Now lying in bed I could only get glimpses of those other worlds, yet somehow I knew that they were real. What stuck was the "feeling" of the dream. It was very real. It happened.

Fred and Dorge were gone when I came back out of my room so I made a fire, fixed some dinner and sat in front of the fire's warmth. A lot had taken place today, and I felt humbled and blessed to be here in this situation with Fred and Dorge, experiencing things I never dreamed were possible. Something had shifted inside me. I no longer was the same David that arrived here such a short time ago. My eyes had been opened as if they had been always closed up till now. I wondered where this journey would end.

✳CHAPTER ELEVEN

Fred said it was now time to complete my mask. I was ready to apply some of the lessons that I had realized.

Since the main features of the mask were now nearing completion, it was time to hollow out the back of the mask. After carefully drawing in the guidelines on the back, I used the adze to remove the wood, being careful not to go too deep; otherwise I would break through to the face side.

I made frequent use of a pair of calipers to measure the depth. After getting close to where I wanted to be I switched to the crooked knife to finish hollowing out the back.

Next I turned the mask over and cut through the mouth, nose and eye openings, taking my time and cutting in the right area. I made use of a gouge for a lot of this work.

Working on the mask was a very grounding experience, which focused my concentration and energy. Often I could feel energy circulating between the mask and myself, similar to what I felt when Fred had his hands on my shoulders. I had few thoughts while I worked.

Time passed unnoticed. I worked in the rhythm of my breath.

Once the openings had been made it was time to thin out more of the mask on the back again. The trick was not to go too deeply or too thin. Since the mask was to be worn, it had to be light, yet strong. Fred taught me to always work both sides at this point to refine the proper opening locations and degree of thickness.

Fred was never very far away while I carved, often sitting down next to me with a similar piece of wood, demonstrating the technique and the best way to proceed. He had many examples, too, of each step that needed to be accomplished. My mask was by no means perfect. In fact, it looked crude compared to anything he had carved. Fred reminded me that the point wasn't to achieve a pretty mask but rather to experience the process, and to let what I had realized work its way into the mask. My technique would improve over time. What was important now was allowing the energy to flow, between me and the piece of red cedar. I took my time, often stopping to practice on a scrap piece of wood before continuing. After a week I was ready to paint my mask.

During this time Dorge was either in the mountains or in town. When he was around, though, I felt a bond with him, and began believing that it might be true that somehow we were from the same soul group. One night I finally got the chance to tell him about the dream I had with him in it. He laughed and said it took lots of energy directing me to that experience.

"I don't understand. You directed my dream?"

"If you recall I excused myself and went to use Fred's little copper shielded room."

"And?"

"I was out and about and noticed that you were lapsing in and out of deep sleep so I invited you to join me out in the desert. Once there, I called upon our other friends to come join us."

"You know Fred said that you and I, Fred and even Natasha are part of the same soul group. So the other people in the dream were also part of our group, right?" I asked.

" Yes, that's correct. Keep up your practice to be more conscious in your dreams and then you will be able to direct what happens instead of just reacting to whatever the mind throws at you. The goal is to be aware and present, whether the body is awake and active, or asleep and refreshing itself."

Fred said before I applied paint to my mask he wanted me to experience the different energies that make up colors. He asked if I liked to take pictures in color or did I prefer black and white. I told him I shot almost entirely in color, that it was more of an emotional experience than black and white. "Yes, but have you really experienced a pure single color with that emotion?" he asked.

"I am not sure, can you explain it further?"

"Think of a very pure red, similar to a fire truck. What does that feel like to you?"

I closed my eyes and thought of the red, trying to

feel the color as Fred suggested. I told him the color felt active, exciting and had movement to it.

"Good, but how does it affect your body?"

Again I concentrated on the color red but realized my mind was just thinking about it, I didn't really have an experience of it. Fred said that was because we take colors for granted and don't realize how those colors really affect us. He said we are attracted to some colors more than others, because our subconscious filters out the effects of the ones that we had disturbing experiences with at an early age. He suggested we go visit the copper room so that he could show me what he was trying to convey. Before we went into his room, it occurred to me that Fred seldom wore a shirt, coat, or pants that was made up of more than one color. No prints or patterns, preferring instead to pick single colors. I had asked him about this once. He just said that was one way to attract what it was he needed to connect with. At the time I didn't give it much thought, seeing how I was preoccupied already with so much to study.

Once in the copper room, Fred instructed me to just lie down, relax and put myself into a receptive state. While I did this, Fred left, only to return shortly with several different colored light bulbs. First he put in a red bulb. The little room now glowed with a red atmosphere. Fred said to imagine breathing in the red color while keeping my eyes open.

"Visualize it spreading throughout your entire body," he said.

I did this for ten minutes or so, and then he said

I could now close my eyes and continue to visualize the color red entering my body. After a while I grew tired of the practice, having had little or no experience. Fred said that he would introduce the sound that matched the color red. I put on headphones and tried again. At first I could only hear a single tone but after a few minutes I noticed that the tone began to multiply, and suddenly I could see the color dancing around in my vision. I could also "feel" the color. It kept moving faster until it felt like my entire body was vibrating at some incredible rate.

Then, I was overcome with a flood of emotions. I felt my muscles tightening and relaxing in quick succession. One minute I felt anger then the next instant unbelievably powerful and dominating. Sexual feelings cursed through my body. Images of red energy swirling and moving at incredible speed passed before me in my mind's eye. Had I become the color, the sound? I couldn't tell. I felt invincible though; I knew this was the raw energy of the universe, undifferentiated and creative. Soon the tone slowed way down and with it the mad onslaught of images and feelings. The tone stopped and I heard Fred's voice, "Come back when you are ready and open your eyes."

I opened my eyes but remained motionless. I could still feel the color's affect. My body felt weak as if I had just run a race. Fred had turned out the red light so it was dark, but I kept seeing hazy images of a red glow.

"Take your time," Fred said, "you'll soon feel normal."

"That was almost too much," I replied. " It felt like

the color would consume me."

"What you experienced was the primal energy in all things, the driving force behind all movement. It's the power within the tender and fragile single blade of grass, pushing up through concrete with unstoppable expansion."

Fred put the white light back in, and asked if I was ready to experience another color.

"Ahhh.... not right now Fred, I think that will do. Maybe later," I replied, still shaken.

"You were right, I've never really felt what colors were till now. Are they all so violent?"

A week went by before Fred said I was ready to experience the other colors. Green was continually changing forms that grew in complexity. Unlike the rapid and explosive nature of red, the green light and sound was soothing and peaceful. I felt the transformational power that brought all things into balance and harmony. I could feel places in my body that were out of alignment and were brought back into balance.

Blue . . . at first I became very sad and reflective as I let the blue light wash over me with my eyes open. Childhood memories filled my mind with scenes of sadness; a lost pet, the death of my sister. When I closed my eyes and went deeper, my sadness grew to grief for all the suffering in the world. I felt the weight of a huge blue vastness compressing my being. When I thought I could no longer bear the weight, it lifted, and my awareness began to expand outward in all directions. The sound became higher pitched until all sadness and grief disappeared and I was then filled with compassion. I was in a vast blue sea and knew that all suffering would eventually be healed, that it would be replaced with acceptance and understanding. I was consumed by an overwhelming sense of joy.

Yellow . . . the yellow light and sound put me in the realm of the mental. I found it difficult to relax; my mind was bombarded with thoughts that came at an alarming rate. I felt restless, and my attempts to let go only allowed more thoughts to intrude upon my space. Finally, after much effort, my mind slowed down and I experienced gaps in my thinking where it was calm and I seemed to float in a dimension occupied by little yellow lights, that would suddenly enter my consciousness, as many thoughts connected together in an idea. I found it difficult to explain to Fred afterwards.

"You were close to entering the Akashic Records, where every thought or idea is stored. You encountered thought forms, little energy bundles made up of related thoughts," he explained.

Of all the colors I experienced, purple was the most interesting and satisfying. As I went deeper into the sound and color, I had a similar experience like the one with Dorge in the clearing. A feeling of oneness and completion engulfed me. An indescribable peace flowed through me. I felt like all was right and in perfect harmony within and without. For days after that I was left in a serene and peaceful mood.

Fred said that unlike the color red, that needed maximum form to express itself, purple needed a minimum form to express its maximum energy.

What I learned was that colors affect us all the time and on many levels, but we aren't conscious of our response so we can't use them directly for our advantage. We can pick certain colors for healing, for mental states, for moods, and for creativity. We can use colors to attract or to repel.

Finally I was given the go-ahead to paint my mask. Fred recommended certain colors for the various parts of the face and showed me examples. The first step was to sand the mask completely smooth and then apply linseed oil mixed with turpentine. After that dried I had to pencil in where the different paints belonged.

Fred cautioned me not to apply the paint too thick; otherwise the wood grain wouldn't show through.

Black was the first color I used, highlighting around the eyes, nose and mouth. Next came red and blue to apply to the same areas inside the black highlighting. The other colors used were yellow and white. Fred hovered over me, giving out advice—more paint here, watch the build up there. The process was not only exciting but also very satisfying. By early afternoon I applied the last few brush strokes.

My first mask was now completed.

Fred appeared excited, congratulating me with a big hug and a slap on the back.

"When Dorge gets back from town he'll be surprised," I said.

"Oh, I imagine you'll be too," he answered grinning.

I wondered what he meant by that, but I was too excited to bother asking.

Fred took the mask and propped it up in the middle of the table, then cleared off everything else. He seemed prouder of the finished mask than I was. As we sat and chatted about the various forms a mask can take, the front door swung open and Dorge walked in.

"Your timing is impeccable," I said.

"Actually Fred's is," he replied.

I started to ask Fred about that when in walked Natasha and Helen.

"Surprise!" they shouted in unison.

I was floored, and looked at Fred with a question in my eyes, who, with a spontaneous gesture, threw his arms out wide, "Time to celebrate!" he said.

After giving everyone a hug I helped Natasha with her bulging pack that held food and drink for the occasion. "How did you know that I would finish?" I asked.

"Dorge and Fred kept a watchful eye out for this day and so here we are," she answered, kissing my cheek.

"Well I can see you have been paying attention to your lessons David," Helen remarked, inspecting the mask. "Can it talk?" she asked.

I couldn't help but laugh, remembering when Paul asked Fred if his mask could speak. Fred must have known what I was laughing at because he told Helen, "It all depends on who's listening."

"What's that suppose to mean, dear?" she replied, "I can hear just fine."

Fred and I continued to laugh. Soon Dorge and Natasha joined in.

"Am I missing something here?" Helen pleaded, looking bewildered.

"It's nothing Helen, just a joke. Get over here and help me set the food out, and I'll explain," Natasha shouted from the kitchen.

Before long, snacks, cheeses and various dips were put on the table along with a few bottles of wine. I was given the task of opening the wine and serving it. I asked for a head count. Who wanted wine? All hands went up. "Fred, I didn't think you drank."

"On special occasions I'll have some, and this is a special occasion now, I think. Right Dorge?" Fred said, giving him a wink.

"I've always heard that the middle way is best, and a glass of wine is good for your blood," he replied grinning.

I just shook my head and poured them a glass. Maybe advanced spiritual teachers like them aren't affected, but I wasn't worrying about it, I was starting to have a great time.

Plates of food found their way to the table: salmon, crab, rice, salad, potatoes, vegetables and deserts. I hadn't seen that much food for two months.

"A toast," announced Helen. "Here's to good friends, good times, and one great mask carver."

"Music!" smiled Natasha, "I brought some CDs along, and Fred, can you pull out that old player you have?"

The mood turned festive: glasses clinking, plates full, and music mingling with the conversation. It felt like Thanksgiving and perhaps it was. I had a lot to be thankful for. My stay here would end soon and I would be heading back to Seattle. By the time I had my third glass of wine, thoughts of home were lost in the merriment of the moment. The party carried on. I awoke in the middle of the night to go relieve myself outside. Natasha was fast asleep next to me and on the way out I noticed Helen sleeping on the floor in a heap of blankets and pillows. Dorge was in his usual place on the couch. The night was clear and I was greeted by a star-filled sky. An owl hooted in the distance, then a brilliant shooting star crossed the dark sky. I would miss this place and my friends. I had connected with nature in a way I never thought possible. I wondered how I would feel surrounded by a city once more. One thing was for sure. I wasn't the same person who left it two months ago.

In the morning, with the exception of Helen, everyone was feeling little or no effects from the party.

"Even though my head feels like a spider built cobwebs there in the middle of the night, I am glad I came. It was a great time," Helen said, who was gathering up her things.

Natasha and I spent time early in the morning talking on the deck. I told her of my plans to go back to Seattle later next week, and hoped she would come visit. She said she would like that as soon as she could get time off. I felt like we had made a solid connection and I began to see us together in the future. I said I would say goodbye in town before leaving.

The day was overcast, but no rain was in sight. Fred suggested we accompany Dorge to a location that he liked, saying he wanted to demonstrate something to me. After an hour of up and down hiking we came to a rocky outcropping at the base of a large mound of rocks. At the top was a spacious flat area. We headed up in that direction. Fred and Dorge led the way, scrambling over boulders with me in fast pursuit. Near the top, the only way to continue was to squeeze past two large rocks. They both made it through and waited as I turned side-ways and inched my way past. Soon we were standing on top of huge flat rocks that commanded a 360-degree view of the surrounding forest. It was breathtaking. Wisps of fog drifted slowly through the trees far below. We sat down and looked at the dramatic sight.

"Everything you see," Dorge said, making a sweeping gesture, "is vibrating, but we only experience a narrow band that our senses can pick up. Our normal perception only experiences a very small part of the world around us. But as you have discovered, David, once we know how to enlarge it, our perception isn't limited to just a narrow band of vibrating energy."

"That's true. Thanks to you and Fred, I've learned to perceive differently."

"Yes, but did you know that you may also change your own rate of vibration to such a degree that others can't even see you?"

I asked him to explain it more, but instead of an-swering, Dorge crossed his legs and sat very straight with his eyes closed. I looked at Fred who motioned to me to remain quiet. I waited and continued to observed Dorge who sat perfectly still, now looking more like a stone sculpture frozen in place.

The shrill cry of a hawk overhead distracted me and I looked up. The hawk was looking down at us, hovering in a place high above. I looked back over to Dorge but he was gone! I quickly looked in all directions, then jumped to my feet and looked the way we had come up through the rocks. I could hear Fred laughing at my sudden bewilderment.

"Fred! Where did he go? He just vanished!" I exclaimed, dismayed and shocked. Fred was beside himself laughing.

"Damn it Fred, this isn't funny! I just looked away for a second or two."

"Calm down David. He's right here, you just can't see him."

"Can't see him? There's no place to hide. Look!" I said, turning around in all directions.

"I suggest you sit down, remain calm, and observe the spot where you last saw him."

I sat down, but felt anxious. Fred pointed to where Dorge had been sitting, and said to keep my attention on that spot.

In a few moments a grayish image appeared where Dorge had been sitting, then, a split second later his finite self was sitting as before; still with eyes closed and sitting like a statue. I reeled back in horror. My brain didn't want to accept what my eyes saw. I started to shake and my mouth became so dry I had difficulty swallowing. I then started to feel sick to my stomach.

"Squeeze your hands and curl your toes rapidly," Fred said, "keep your attention on your breath and center yourself."

I did as he instructed and soon felt better.

"Like I was saying, you can change your own vibration so that others can't see you," Dorge said, giving his body a quick shake and stretching his arms out to his sides. "I realize it is bit of a shock for the mind to witness such a thing for the first time."

"Dorge! That scared the crap out of me! Did you really disappear?"

"Do you want me to do it again?"

"No! No, I believe you, trust me—it's just that I wasn't expecting that. My mind sort of went numb. What did you do? Where did you go?"

"I apologize if you felt discomfort. When the mind comes up empty with a logical explanation, it sometimes goes into panic mode. As you might have guessed, I didn't really go anywhere. I just increased my rate of vibration until you no longer could perceive me. The more difficult task was to get that hawk to hover above us to get your attention!" he replied grinning. "I am afraid Fred's more gifted in that department."

I asked Fred if he could disappear also.

"No, not yet, but I am working on it," he answered with a big grin.

"Learning to access powers isn't the reason to achieve these things," Dorge said. They are gifts, if you will, for letting go of our false ego and striving for self-realization."

We sat quietly for a long period enjoying the view and our own private thoughts. It took a long time before I felt completely calm again. We decided to head back, as the air had turned chilly and a light drizzle was beginning to fall.

❋CHAPTER TWELVE

My ferry back to Seattle would arrive on the week-end. I spent my last few days with Fred discussing plans to come back and continue my studies with him. He said that when I return to Seattle it will take a while to adjust to my "old life," and not to neglect my practices. He said that if I did, I would slide back into old patterns. He also advised that I take back a large piece of cedar to carve another mask on my own, so that I wouldn't forget the skills that I had learned.

He hoped that I would continue to practice the out-of-body lessons, even though I wouldn't have the benefit of his copper room. "The protection from your ego will be in your practice, please take it to heart," adding, "If you can afford it, you can even turn a closet into a little copper room."

He reminded me to always use the protective shield that he had shown me before attempting any out-of-body techniques. The shield was a visualized egg-like ring that surrounded the body, an energy shield, as he called it. I was to always visualize this shield of energy surrounding me before I practiced leaving my body just in case "lower entities" tried to disturb me.

I still felt a slight fear whenever I practiced leaving my body. Fred said with experience that would disappear, and eventually I would be able to visit him when I perfected the technique. He said that no harm could come to a person who was "out exploring" even though I might encounter things that frightened me. Of course that induced a sense of fear right away! I trusted Fred and his judgment, and knew he wouldn't ask me to practice something that could be harmful.

My bags were packed and piled near the front door when it suddenly hit me. Today I was leaving Fred's world! I would dearly miss Fred and this beautiful place.I would also miss Dorge, with whom I had developed a strong connection.

As usual Fred picked up on my mood.

"Don't worry you'll do just fine, you have now planted some deep roots that can keep you anchored along your path, as long as you do your part."

Dorge gave me a big hug, saying, "Now that the door is open, enjoy the journey. Don't make a big deal of it or your ego will jump right in there. Just do your practices and a solid momentum will build."

Tears came to my eyes when I hugged Fred.

"Remember to use what you know, and feel your feet once in a while," he said smiling with a gentle and soft tone.

Soon I was out the door and headed across the meadow. I stopped and turned to give a last wave goodbye. Fred and Dorge were standing on the deck waving back.

As I walked along, two crows cawed loudly overhead. I hollered up to them, "Tell Fred I'll be back soon." When I arrived in Bella Namu, I booked a room at the Cedar Inn, took a shower, and then went to the Raven's Nest. Natasha and Helen were both there.

"So you're on your way back to the big city. We're going to miss you around here," Helen said, pouring me some coffee.

"I am going to miss you too, Helen, and when I return you'd better still be here."

"Honey, I'll probably be here till the good Lord lets me know otherwise," she answered, then leaned over to whisper, "Rumor has it that Natasha is going to visit you."

"I hope you're right Helen," I whispered back.

Soon Natasha appeared, "I can't believe you're leaving already, seems like you just got here."

"I know, I am starting to miss everyone and I haven't even left yet! Now remember, you're coming to see me as soon as you get the time, right?"

"I can't wait. It's starting to slow down here and soon it will mostly be locals. I'll come see you then."

Natasha spent the night with me one last time. Before I knew it we were saying goodbye at the ferry terminal. We held one another till the last call to board was given and then I made my way to the back of the ferry, and watched till Bella Namu was just a speck in the distance.

❋CHAPTER THIRTEEN

My apartment had shrunk, or so it seemed. The spaces in my head were bigger now, and the apartment felt cramped and confining. It seemed all my reference points had shifted. It felt as if I had been away for years. I saw things with different eyes. A clarity had replaced the routine that had put me to sleep before. People seemed to continually be in high gear and distracted. Seattle felt chaotic and speeded up.

I could feel my body and mind also speeding up, yet something inside remained a calm refuge from daily life. I still felt the momentum I had built up at Fred's, but it was now being challenged, so I doubled my efforts to stick to my daily check-in process.

The contrast between living at Fred's and living at home was fast becoming obvious. I would catch myself looking at my watch for no other reason than I was wearing it again. Up north everything moved at a slower pace, and the in-the-moment experience was the norm at Fred's. Back here in Seattle, the clock was king. Life revolved around measured time. I kept remembering what Fred had told me, *"Keep up your practices, otherwise you will slide back into old patterns."*

Now I knew why people sought out the solitude of mountains, deserts and the quiet places—there were fewer distractions.

I was determined not to fall back into old patterns, so I scheduled all appointments and work after 10:00 AM in the morning. I even made coffee at home, instead of rushing off to Java Junky. I kept the mornings for grounding and getting centered and focused before I entered "the mind's arena."

On the weekends I took the time to focus even more on things that I had learned, often going into the mountains seeking out a quiet place. Aside from practicing the sensing of energy fields and averted seeing, I practiced feeling the energy between my palms until I could do it easily. Next, I practiced shaping it into a ball as Fred had done and visualized tossing it around, but found this was still difficult to do. After much practice I could toss it up out of my hands and feel it come back down.

John was delighted to see the mask I had carved.

"So you *did* do something up there after all that time! Not bad. You actually did a great job for your first attempt. I doubt if I could have done any better," he commented, putting the mask on and clowning around, "Hey, can I use this for Halloween?"

"Very funny," I replied, taking back the mask.

"Okay, so tell me about the lessons you learned."

As best I could, I explained some of the things that I practiced. Of course he was skeptical. "Do you really believe all those things?"

"John, I experienced them. They weren't made up

in my head. Here I'll show you something," I said. Asking him to take hold of my hand, I concentrated on sending energy to him.

Almost immediately he jerked his hand away. "Wow! How did you do that?"

I laughed at his sudden reaction, "John, come on, I am not going to shock you, just hold my hand for a few seconds."

Again I sent energy through his hand. "Do you feel it get warmer and a mild tingling sensation?" I asked.

"Yeah, yeah, weird, what are you doing?"

I explained what was going on, that it is possible to channel energy through us.

"That's neat, but what does that have to do with carving a mask?"

"It means we can also channel that same energy into the wood that we are carving, that the wood can be infused with our own energy signature, if you will. That's why I could have the experience I told you about at the gallery with Fred's mask."

"David, you know I've worked with wood for a long time now, and I never once felt anything but wood grain and how dense it is. You're saying that somehow you can put energy into that stuff? Do I look stupid?"

"No you're not stupid, but there are a lot of things that we don't understand about this world around us. For one thing, solid wood is really just atoms—with a whole lot of space in between. As a matter of fact it's mostly empty space."

"Yeah I know, all that science stuff, but my senses

say it's solid and that's how I make my living. But you know, if I learn this technique, then I could put energy into my furniture, and sell it for ten times the amount, right?" he said grinning.

"Right, John,"

I demonstrated how to feel energy between your palms, slowly bringing the palms together. After awhile I could see John becoming more interested in what I was explaining. "You know, maybe it was a good thing you went to study with this guy, you seem calmer and more focused. You're going to have to show me more of this stuff."

While we talked an idea came to mind. "Hey listen, how would you like to rent me a little space over in one corner of your shop?"

"Heck, I've got plenty of space here. What do have in mind?"

I explained to John about Fred's copper-shielded room.

"Look I know you experienced a lot of things up there and it all sounds interesting, but a copper room?"

"It's a place to meditate, visualize, things like that. The copper acts like a shield to block out electrical currents and other outside influences."

"Look, it's fine with me if you want to build this thing, just don't ask me to test it out. I am happy to just make things out of wood."

Days turned into weeks and I was beginning to miss Fred and Natasha. I still hadn't heard from either of them and I began to get concerned when a letter finally arrived from Natasha. She was sorry she had not written but was busy working as much as she could to save money for a visit here. If things went as planned she would be here in about two weeks. She said that she would call me on a certain date and time and I made sure I wrote it down. She said that Fred and Dorge had gone off to Tibet. Fred didn't know when he would return, but he would be in touch. The news left me in a sad mood for some reason. He was no longer only a days journey away, but thousands of miles away, somewhere in Tibet. I realized then how much I missed his presence.

Fred did indeed keep in touch—through a lucid dream I had. "Look at your hands and know that this is real, David," he said in the dream. We were in a forest somewhere; a crow was on his shoulder. When he said this I looked at my hands and suddenly my awareness dramatically increased and I knew that I was out of my body, which was asleep in my apartment. I looked around and realized that we were back in the forest near Fred's house.

"Fred, I am awake. I mean I am here just like when I am in my body!" I said excitedly.

"This is how we stay in touch. I am here to remind you that you must keep up the practice. How is the copper room coming together?"

"The copper room! Yes, I am going to build one in my friend's workspace."

"Fred, where are you living now?"

"Would you like to see?"

"How? Where?"

Fred took my hand and said to gaze into his eyes. In a flash we were high in the mountains somewhere. Snow was falling. I looked at Fred and then at myself but no snow was hitting us. "We're in the Astral dimension. We are invisible to the physical world," Fred said.

"Then why can I see you and myself? We have bodies."

"These are for convenience. Our awareness is projecting them; just like all the physical matter you see in your normal earthly state. Come, let me show you where I live."

Fred led the way down a path and we came to two huts made out of stone. Fred said to look inside, but to not touch anything, especially his body that was asleep!

I went inside and saw a form lying down on a bed of straw and covered with many blankets. I didn't have the courage to look closer. "Is that you?" I asked in disbelief after hurriedly coming back out.

"I think so, last time I checked." he replied laughing. "Dorge is off gathering yak dung. Before we go find him I want to show you something."

Fred took me by the arm and led me just inside his stone hut, and then he pointed to a large round bowl sitting on top of a table. "Soon you will be able to use that bowl to give yourself a boost in your training."

"How?"

"When it is correctly played, it will sing your vibration, your own particular energy signature. Now let's go find Dorge."

We found Dorge walking with a basket full of

dung, which was used for fuel. I went up to him with greetings. He didn't respond but continued to walk right through me. Fred was bent over double with laughter.

"Have you forgotten that you're on another plane here?" he hollered.

"Oh yeah, that's right. Does he know we are here?"

Before Fred could answer, Dorge put the basket down and appeared to sniff the air and slowly looked around, then got a big grin on his face.

"Okay Fred, now why don't you get back in your body so you can help me with these chores. Say, who do you have with you anyway? Feels familiar."

Dorge picked up his basket and continued back to the huts. Fred said that when he got back he would no doubt wake him and then he wouldn't be here with me anymore.

"But Fred, what do I do?" I asked alarmed.

Fred slapped his hands together with a great force, and shouted, "Wake up!"

I woke up with a sudden urgency, breathing heavily. I could still feel the jolt of reentering my body as if the alignment was off somewhat.

I got up and wrote down what had taken place while it was still fresh in my memory. It had been so vivid that I had no problem recalling every detail. I was convinced that it was real, that it all took place as I slept. Yet, upon waking, I wasn't so sure. I decided that the only way to find out once and for all, was to get the copper room built, get over my fear, and learn to travel.

✳CHAPTER FOURTEEN

My work in photography began to change. I started seeing into the connectedness of things on a higher level. Before, I would just sense that there was an underlying connection between things, but now I could actually "see" a flow of energy moving between elements in a landscape. I would get so carried away with what I was experiencing that I had to put the camera down and just experience the flow. I wondered if photography could still hold the same interest it once did.

Commercial and editorial assignments were always the work that brought in steady lucrative jobs, but even those were losing my interest. In the past, I never gave much thought about how my work was used to sell products. But now I saw it could actually keep people addicted to their conditioned selves.

I didn't really realize how much I had changed till I came back and lived in the "market place" again.

I started to experience two distinct sides to myself: One was transcendental, the other physical. The transcendental was the soul connected to the heart, the gateway beyond time and space. The physical was the body connected to the senses, limited by time and space.

My former conditioning acted like filters that kept me from experiencing the transcendental. It was only when the lessons that Fred taught me began to bear fruit that those filters started to weaken and I began to experience the present moment in greater depth, where pleasure and pain were replaced with a deep satisfaction in whatever I was focused on. It could be as mundane as putting gas in my car, or waiting in line at the post office and I would be in a state of bliss.

I also discovered that when I dwelt on the past or became concerned about the future those blissful moments disappeared quickly. It was only when I was fully present that I had an opportunity to experience higher states of joy.

After locating where to purchase copper sheets and the necessary building materials, John and I jumped into his truck and went on a shopping spree.

"Are you sure this copper room you're building is safe and won't make you eventually go mad?" John said, twisting up his face.

I laughed, "Now that is the face of one crazy man. Our little room does just the opposite—it takes your madness away."

"If you say so, but like I said, don't ask me to try it out."

"Oh, you're starting to like this idea, aren't you, John?"

"Hey, how can I like something I know nothing about? Besides, I already said that you won't get me in there."

"You know I've never seen you act so strange about something that is no big deal. What freaks you out so much about this copper room anyway?"

John became lost in thought for a while.

"When I was young my mom used to play with a Ouiji board. She would freak me out saying she could talk with people that were dead. That's why I avoid that kind of stuff."

"That's it, an experience when you were young and your mother's Ouiji board?"

"Well, I do think I saw a ghost standing behind my Mom one time and the lights kept flickering on and off. I am telling you it freaked me out."

We didn't talk about it after that. With John's help it only took two weeks to build a small room, complete with copper sheeting, ten feet by four feet. I decided that I could use flashlights and a CD player instead of wiring the tiny room. When the door was finally attached, I told John to just stick his arm through the door and tell me if he felt anything different.

"Whoa! That's the strangest sensation I've ever felt," he said, yanking his arm back.

"If you go in and shut the door, no outside electrical or other influences can enter, sort of like a vacuum."

John hesitated but finally caved in to his curiosity. He went inside and shut the door. He came out wide-eyed and excited. "I swear I could hear my mind thinking. That was a terrific feeling. Talk about a soundproof room."

"It's a great place to calm down and turn inward.

Living in a city we are always bombarded with a jumble of electrical signals and random thoughts, but in there you can be totally isolated from them and get into a deeper and quieter place."

After I installed a small bed I told John he was welcome to use the room anytime. He said he never learned to meditate but perhaps I could show him some simple techniques to quiet the mind. His interest amazed me because never before had he shown the slightest interest in self-improvement or any kind of spirituality. I told him I would welcome the chance to share what I knew.

Now that the room was completed, I decided to begin another mask with the wood Fred sent home with me. I first had to soak it for a few days to make it easier to carve, and next I needed to pencil in an outline to work from. I paid a visit to the new room. I needed to visualize a new face.

After two visits I had a vision of the next mask. Unlike my first mask, this face was older and more Caucasian appearing. There was something about it that was very familiar, but I couldn't put my finger on why. When it first appeared I thought that it was the face of someone that I knew, but I didn't know who. I had no problem in sketching it afterwards, the face being so familiar. It was almost like a feeling of deja vu.

John looked over my shoulder after the sketch was finished and asked if it was someone I knew. "Not really, I mean the face sure reminds me of someone but I don't know who—yet."

"You know," said John, "I think it looks like you

only much older."

As soon as he said that I got goose bumps. It did remind me of myself, sort of. The more I looked at the drawing the more I became convinced that indeed I somehow had a vision of myself as an old man. Both John and I were amazed. "You said it just came to you while you were in the room?" John asked.

"Not exactly. The way it works is I first bring myself into a receptive state and then sort of wait for a vision to appear."

"Well, I guess you'll be carving a mask that is you around eighty years old. Hey, I know, you could take it on dates to show them how you look in the future!"

"Very funny," I replied, "I'll have to ask Fred what this means. After all, maybe it's a good thing."

John just gave me a sideward glance as if to say yeah, right. That night in a dream Fred told me, "Go visit the gallery tomorrow."

I woke with those words still fresh in my mind. I don't remember seeing him in my dream, but I knew it was his voice. I was somewhere in the mountains when I heard him say it twice. It was so vivid that I canceled an appointment with a new client. It would be the first time I had returned to the gallery since I last saw Fred there.

I felt excited, yet a little apprehensive when I arrived at the gallery door. Maybe because I didn't know why I should be there. What if the dream was just that— a dream without any real message? Upon entering I felt a deep sense of peace spread through me, and my apprehension left.

"Welcome, David." Paul said walking up, "It has been too long. How are you?"

"Just great Paul. It really feels good to be back here," I answered giving him a hug. "How are things?"

"Couldn't be better. We're so glad you could make it."

"We? Did you know I was coming in today?"

Paul smiled, "Come I want you to see an old friend."

We entered a room at the back of the gallery. The lights were turned down low and many large candles were lit which made it difficult to see in the room. Then I noticed someone sitting at a table toward the back of the room. As I came closer the person lifted his head.

"Dorge! What are you doing here? I thought you were in Tibet!"

Getting up and giving me a welcome embrace, he said that he needed to come back, and that Fred had asked him to look me up. "I have something to give to you from Fred," he said, pointing to a large bowl on the nearby table.

When I saw the bowl I remembered my dream where Fred had pointed out a bowl saying that I would make use of it someday.

I told Dorge about my dream.

"Oh, I was out collecting yak dung right?"

"Yes! But he also pointed out a bowl in one corner of his place. Is that it?"

He didn't answer but went over and brought the bowl back, laying it on the table. "I am pretty sure this is what you saw. It is called a singing bowl, hand made. You can see the hammer marks on the outside. This particular bowl is very special because it has two tones, one high and the other low."

"It's beautiful," I said. "What is it used for?"

"See for yourself," he replied, taking a round wooden baton and running it along the outside rim of the bowl. Almost at once a beautiful resonating sound could be heard. "Now close your eyes and let the sound go deep inside you."

I closed my eyes and listened to the sound, which indeed had a high and low tone. The sound washed over me, taking with it all the random thoughts that only a moment before had cluttered my mind. The volume of sound seemed to expand and with it my awareness. I felt like I had entered a huge open space of clarity and focus. I was filled with a feeling of peace as the sound resonated in waves within the space I now occupied. Before long I couldn't distinguish between myself and the sound. There seemed to be no difference.

Dorge stopped using the baton and the sound faded out slowly. I could still hear it minutes later, very faintly. I opened my eyes. "That's got to be one of the most beautiful and inspiring sounds, I ever heard. I felt like I was vibrating with it at the same rate."

"You were. The tones match your own vibration. Using this before you meditate or do any inner work will help you to bypass the busyness of the mind. Fred had it especially made for you. Use it on a daily basis, when you wake up and before going to sleep."

I didn't know what to say. I kept thinking, 'why is all this happening to me?' A short time ago I was just doing what I had always been doing for years, and then I walk into a gallery and my life gets turned around so that I see the world with new eyes.

"Dorge, I am curious, does Fred give this much attention to all his students, even after they leave?"

"It all depends. If there is a sincere desire to apply the knowledge that is offered and the timing is right then, yes, Fred will always be there for that person. As our energy changes we will also attract people that become our next chapter along the path. Then again, if we don't take the gifts given to heart we will remain in our conditioned selves and again attract people that hold us back."

"I just feel so fortunate to have come into this gallery and met Fred. Was it destiny?"

"Let's just say that the seeds you have sown are now beginning to bear fruit. That's all."

Sometime during our conversation I mentioned that my new mask drawing looked a lot like myself. Dorge's face turned serious, "How old did the face look?"

"Well, that's the strange part. It looked like me if I were really old, maybe in my seventies or eighties."

His serious look turned into a frown, then, just as fast, returned to a smiling Dorge.

"Is there something bad about that?" I asked, somewhat alarmed.

His eyes softened, his face looking angelic. "Life has many twists and turns, we must do our best to stay the course and remain in the present moment where all things are possible." He then looked away, as if in deep thought, slowly stroking his chin, finally he turned back, "What you drew might have been your death mask."

His words felt like a lightening bolt striking the ground a few feet away. "Death mask! Are you saying I'm going to die?" I knew he wasn't joking, he said it with such sincerity.

"Aren't we all? Only the Great Ones know the day they will depart. Perhaps you just got an early warning, I wouldn't give it too much thought though, you could have another fifty years before your day arrives."

It didn't matter what he said. I was shocked. I asked him what if I didn't carve it?

"You must," he said emphatically. " We have to honor death as much as we embrace life. Life and death are as bride and groom; their union is what gives us all a chance to realize what is beyond this illusion."

I suddenly became very sad and felt empty inside. I thought back to my parents' death, which had always haunted me. Now the memory was back as if it were only yesterday. I was only ten when they died in a plane crash. Death was something that I tried to keep pushed out of my mind. I was raised by my uncle until I left at eighteen, but it became obvious that I never got over their sudden departure from my life.

Dorge no doubt felt my sudden mood shift and the long face. "I want to give you a daily practice that will dispel negative thoughts about death. If you practice this, you will find an inner strength that will take hold." I took a big breath, relaxed and then gave Dorge my full attention. He said that the technique was practiced in Tibet, by those who understood that death is a doorway we shouldn't fear or run from. It was to our advantage to embrace our final conclusion in this life, as consciously as we could.

He said to begin each day by first using the singing bowl, letting the sound settle into my being, while I did my breathing exercises. Once centered and grounded firmly, I was to visualize taking one last breath in, then on the exhale to visualize a great white light enveloping my being. I should tell myself that I have left my body for good, that it had served its purpose, and I would now, once more, return to the spirit. Doing this exercise daily would take the fear of death away.

I gave it a try but I felt like I was just going through the motions. Something in me still remained numb. Thoughts of doubt kept intruding.

I wasn't going to die anytime soon. Maybe my sketch wasn't a "death mask" anyway. Finally after a few more attempts I told Dorge I was sorry but I just couldn't get into it right now.

He smiled and nodded, then said he realized this might feel like a strange thing to practice but it had many benefits—even if it turned out that the mask I was contemplating was not my death mask.

John came in and joined us and we all chatted while drinking hot tea and munching on rice crackers. When it was time for me to leave, after saying good-bye, I told Dorge I looked forward to our next chance to meet and share knowledge.

"Just take life a day at a time and let the process keep you grounded in the ever present reality of now," Dorge answered.

I began to sketch in the mask a week later after deciding to not change the design. But I still didn't want to accept that this might be a death mask—mine or otherwise.

After penciling the sketch onto the wood, I began to reduce the wet block of cedar until I had the basic rough shape I was after. So that symmetry and balance were maintained, I redrew the outline of the mask frequently. I realized that giving the face the appearance of someone in their seventies or eighties would challenge my skill level.

I decided to take Dorge's advice and practice "seeing" my own death. What surprised me was, that after the first week, the practice actually felt natural. I wasn't bothered by my earlier convention that this was a strange thing to be doing. If anything, it reminded me how great it was to be alive in the here and now.

My life settled back into a routine with work, practice, and carving. I usually managed to spend two hours a day on the various lessons that I practiced.

The weather had turned cold and rainy, so a lot of times I had to practice in my apartment or at John's studio. Although results seemed slow I remembered what Fred had told me, *'Don't look for results, just keep going and enjoy the process'*.

To test my ability to project energy from my palms I used a Ping-Pong ball suspended from a string in my apartment. After much practice I finally succeeded in moving the ball a few inches. At first I couldn't believe I really moved it. I thought for sure an air current had influenced the results. When I moved it a third time I was ecstatic. I couldn't wait to show John. Now he would be a believer, or so I thought.

I set up the experiment for John and tried to move the Ping-Pong ball but nothing happened. I tried again with the same results. I couldn't understand what was different. After many more attempts I gave up.

My failure and disappointment to move the ball any amount was a wakeup call. "Guess it will be a while before you can walk on water," John commented with a smirk.

Fred had cautioned me against showing off the things that I had achieved. *Use whatever powers you possess to help others, and those same powers will continue to help you. Otherwise they could very well be your downfall,* were his words.

I realized that there was a part of me that wanted to do extraordinary things, to be seen as special. That part of course was my ego. If my false self got in the way, I couldn't let go enough to let the energy flow out from my hands. I doubled my efforts to practice this technique in a humbler way. Before long I could move the ball straight out, feeling the force leave my hands. But I decided not to give any more demonstrations to John.

I received word from Natasha that she would be visiting the following week. I scheduled my work so that I could spend as much time as possible with her. Dorge had returned to Tibet, saying that he and Fred wouldn't be back until the spring. He said that I should continue to practice my out-of-body exercises so that I could pay them a visit now and then.

"How would I know where to find you?" I asked.

"All you have to do is think of us and you will instantly be there."

"That's it?"

"Thought is instantaneous, not bound by time and space. Your intent is a direct line. You'll see."

The only time I could practice was at night when John wasn't working. In the daytime John was around and I just couldn't concentrate with all the noise from his wood shop. Of all the things that I had learned, leaving my body was the most difficult. I didn't have the benefit of the sounds Fred played, but at least I had my own copper room.

One technique that I used was to lie comfortably and visualize my body rising up into the sky. Yet another technique was to set an intention to look at my hands in a dream and that would be my cue to become fully conscious in that dream. I soon found that I could practice both of these techniques, even if I couldn't use the copper room.

Natasha finally arrived and we spent the first week just exploring Seattle. It was great to see her, and our relationship began to show signs that we might be partners. The love we shared together felt like it sprang from some deep source, waiting to flow when the time was right. Each day brought us closer together. We had long talks about our lives, and I showed her the singing bowl that Fred had sent with Dorge.

"You saw Dorge?"

"Yes, I was totally surprised to see him. I thought he was in Tibet."

She loved the singing bowl and felt it was a close match for her energy too. I didn't tell her what Dorge had said about my drawing, I didn't want to alarm her. Later that evening while Natasha was in the shower, I called and reserved a table for two at a favorite restaurant.

"I made reservations for dinner at eight." I shouted so she could hear me over the sound of the shower.

"Okay, great. Is it a fancy place or can I dress casually?" she shouted back.

"Casual. It has great Italian food, not too upscale. The only drawback is it's in a part of town that's pretty rundown. But hey, that's where you find some of the best restaurants," I replied, hoping she wouldn't mind the surrounding area.

She soon came out wearing a dress, her hair still wet and fresh from the shower.

"Wow, don't you look sexy. I've never seen you in a dress before," I said.

"Oh, I do have other clothes besides jeans, you know. I felt like dressing up a bit."

"Hey, maybe we should forget the dinner, call up for take out and stay in bed!" I said, feeling frisky.

"No way! You're taking me out to dinner. Besides, there is always after dinner delights you know."

We found the location and parked as close as possible in an alleyway next door to the restaurant. "Are you sure your car will be okay here?" she asked as we walked into the restaurant.

"No problem, I've done it before. It will be fine," I assured her.

As we ate dinner, we enjoyed a long intimate conversation, catching up on our lives since we last saw each other.

"Have you seen your Dad much?"

"Occasionally I run into him in town. You know, after that experience with Fred behind the cafe, he seemed to change."

"How so?"

"He has actually been sober and says hello to me in a sincere, kind way. Maybe he is finally realizing that life is short and perhaps we should show a little kindness."

I could tell that she was happy about this. Her eyes were bright and shiny.

"You're right, David, the food's great, and it's so cozy in here. How did you find this place?"

"My friend John turned me on to it. You haven't met him yet."

"You mentioned him before. He's your best friend, right?"

"I guess so. We go back a long way, but he is really different from me," I answered, pouring some more wine.

"In what way is he different?"

"Well, I wouldn't say he isn't spiritual, but he

wouldn't be into the things we are. John is more down to earth, more of a meat and potatoes kind of guy. But he has a big heart and we have shared some great adventures. In fact people say we look alike. He was teasing me about the sketch I did for a new mask I want to carve."

"New mask?"

"Oh, I didn't tell you, the sketch looks like me, only me about eighty years old."

Natasha became quiet and seemed to be lost in her thoughts. We continued to eat and finally I asked her what she was thinking.

She stared at me a few seconds and then asked me about the sketch I had drawn. "My Dad once said that an old face in a mask was considered a dying or death mask!"

"That's what Dorge called it!" I blurted out.

Natasha stared at me again as if waiting for me to see something.

"David, didn't you just say that John looked like you! Well maybe it's his face that you drew."

A chill went up my spine.

"Can you sketch it on this placemat paper?"

I knew it by heart and quickly sketched in the face that I visualized.

Natasha took the drawing and stared at it for a long time. Then she closed her eyes and sat still. When she finally opened her eyes, tears were forming.

"Natasha, what is it?" I asked, feeling something dreadful was about to happen.

"I shouldn't try and interpret the future, it's just that I get this overpowering feeling that something is going to happen, an accident or something."

"Did you see something? What was it?"

After a long silence she told me that what she saw was an accident of some sorts and that I was distraught over it. Since she didn't know John she couldn't tell if it was he who had the accident.

"Look, let's let go of this stuff for a while. I can't be getting freaked out over the future—I want to enjoy the time we have together, okay?" I said.

"I only told you because I thought you should know. But perhaps you're right, I don't want to think about it either."

By the time we left the restaurant it was late. We walked outside and turned to go down the alley, which was dimly lit. I caught sight of someone in front of my car and as we got closer I saw a shadow, cast by the streetlight behind us, appear suddenly in front of us. The hair stood up on the back of my neck. I whispered to Natasha that we were being followed and not to panic.

A man stepped out from behind my car and walked toward us.

"Stay away from us!" I hollered. By now a second person was coming up fast behind us. I swung around to confront the person behind us. Throwing out my arm I shouted, "Hold it right there!"

"Well, well, Mr. Hero, why don't you just throw your wallet over to us and you both can leave un-harmed," the man behind us said, as he met up with his crony. They took up a position directly across the alley from us. They appeared to be in their twenties; two Latino men about my size.

Natasha grabbed my arm and told me throw my wallet over to them. I hesitated because I sensed that wouldn't be the end of it. I pushed Natasha behind me and told her to be still. I decided that I would gamble on what I had learned. I felt my feet, centered myself, and then opened my hands and concentrated on bringing energy into them.

"You should listen to the smart girl and give us your wallet–now!"

I didn't reply but concentrated on what I had done with the Ping-Pong balls. I could feel the energy running into my hands and out.

"Enough of this shit," one of the men said, pulling out a pocket-knife. I held my hands out toward them. The second man reached into his pocket, and slowly opened his own pocket-knife.

They started laughing at my posture. "Ooh, the Kung Fu master," one of them mocked as they advanced

I projected the energy as best I could. They stopped and with a puzzled look, shook their heads as if they were trying to clear them. I did it again, feeling the flow of energy leave my outstretched palms. Again they appeared to try and shake something off.

"What the fuck is going on? This guy's playing with us," one of them said.

I was beginning to feel very drained of energy and knew that I only had one last try. I projected the energy as forcefully as I could toward the two men. This time they both grabbed their heads, dropping their knives in the process and started muttering something in Spanish. I grabbed Natasha's arm and we ran to the car. As soon as we got in I started it up, sped down the alley, turned onto the main street and drove away fast.

"I've never been so scared in all my life! What did you do?" Natasha said, looking back behind us as we drove away.

"Thank God it worked!" I said, still feeling the adrenaline.

"What worked? What did you do?"

"Remember Fred did the same thing to your Dad and his friend behind the cafe, although much more powerfully?"

"Are you sure? My Dad was knocked down but those guys acted like their minds went berserk or something."

"Their minds were crazy and that's what they experienced. Fred did it to me once, only in a very small dosage. I'll explain it better later, I'm just glad it worked."

"I've parked in that alley a hundred times and never run into a problem," John said after hearing my story. "Here, try it on me, I want to see if my mind goes crazy," he added laughing.

"Forget it, I'm through trying to show off. Besides, you're crazy enough already!"

"Hey, it's about time we go for a coastal paddle. What are you doing this weekend?" John asked.

"John, have you seen the weather report? It's supposed to be windy this weekend and you know how the coast can get."

"Hey, we've had challenging paddles before. Besides you're getting soft. You need the exercise."

I just gave him a incredulous glance, "Off the coast, right? Are you in good enough shape for a beating? How is your Eskimo roll lately?" Our talk turned into a testosterone-fueled debate about bravado, not the rational thinking the paddle required.

"You're the one who would need it, ole buddy. I never fall out of my boat, remember. Look, we'll be fine. If it gets too rough we can just go ashore."

Part of me thought what the heck it would be an adventure, but my intuition said that it could be foolish and dangerous. The open coast wasn't a place to relearn rusty skills if the weather and water turned nasty. I voiced my concerns to John.

"Listen, if you can hold off two dangerous desperadoes with just your open palms surely you can stay in your kayak if the ocean gets choppy! Are you with me or do I have to show up at the kayak store tomorrow with a sign hanging from my neck, 'Who wants to go paddle the coast?'"

"Okay John, but you promise if it gets too dicey we pull out. I'm serious John. Okay?"

"You've got a deal, buddy. I say we launch from Eagle Point and take out at Sandy beach. That would be only eight miles, just an easy three hours of paddling. You know, your new girlfriend could drop us off and then meet us at Sandy Beach."

"That would work. I'll ask her if she'd be willing. You've never met her, so that would work too."

"Hum . . . too bad she doesn't have a beautiful sister along with her—does she?"

Before I left we got out the map of the area and checked for possible landings just in case things got too crazy out there. We both had dry suits and all the emergency gear one would need. Since it was only a half-day's paddle we wouldn't need food except for some energy bars. I planned to pick John up early and drive out to the coast on Saturday.

✳CHAPTER FIFTEEN

Natasha agreed to drive ahead, after we paddled out, and meet us at the designated take-out spot. She was looking forward to meeting John.

We arrived and started unloading our gear. As I thought, the wind was blowing but not too strong. The surf was about four feet and I knew that this was not going to be a walk in the park. John couldn't stop talking with Natasha on the drive out to the beach. He was fascinated with her strong independent streak and the fact she hadn't married yet.

"How does a pretty gal like you keep all that male energy at bay living up in that rugged area?"

"Actually, they get intimidated when they find out I can take care of myself, and I guess I don't put out the vibe that I'm available. Besides, my interests are way different from most everyone I know up there."

"Then why do you stay so far north? Seems you would have a better chance of meeting someone here."

"Well, I finally have," she answered, giving me a kiss on the cheek.

"Oh yeah, I forgot, you're spoken for," John said laughing.

"Don't worry John, you'll find someone when you least expect it," Natasha told him.

"Is that a destiny thing?"

"Woman of your dreams, John," I quipped.

While John was getting his boat ready, Natasha took me aside. "David, I know you two are set on this paddle but be extra cautious, something just doesn't feel right."

"A little late now. I mean, John would really be disappointed. What is it? Is it what you felt at the restaurant?" I asked, searching her expression.

She just looked down at the pavement, shuffling her feet back and forth. I took hold of her shoulders, "Natasha, what is it?"

Finally she looked up, "I just get this intuitive feeling that something is wrong, something bad is going to happen," she answered biting her lip.

"Look, we've made plans to get out of the water the moment it gets too rough. If we don't show up at the spot I told you, it's because we took out at another place and one of us would hitch a ride to where you are. It might take a while but one of us will be there. Relax."

"All right, just be careful. I love you."

"I love you too. Listen, John and I have done this before. We're very good kayakers. Now don't worry."

Once ready, John and I pushed from the sand and paddled fast to make it over and past the breaking waves. Soon we were outside the surf zone and turned the bow of our boats to parallel the coastline. The wind wasn't so bad after all and the cloud cover broke, allowing the sunlight to bounce off the water.

John looked over and smiled, "Now this is what it's all about. Aren't you glad we came?"

"This is great, I thought it would be a lot rougher. It's beautiful out here."

The swell was four to six feet high, lifting our bows up as we paddled at a steady pace. My senses became sharper—the smell of the sea, the feel of the wind on my face. Kayaking in the open ocean was like a dance. Once you learned the steps you could let go to its rhythm. As my paddle sliced through the water I experienced a peace that only the ocean can provide.

One section of our route had lots of jagged rocks and a small shallow reef which, at low tide, would be exposed, making for cautious navigation through it, unless we paddled further out to sea. According to the tide log we would be entering that area at low tide. I pulled up next to John.

"You know the tide is going out and that wicked spot with all the rocks will be exposed to the max."

"Yeah, so, what do you suggest, we go around it?"

"Let's just wait and see."

"Heck, let's really turn this into an adventure and play in the rock gardens!"

"Right, with fiberglass boats! If we had plastic I would say yes. You know what we didn't bring—helmets!"

"Ahh. . . you're right, but you brought the responder, so if you crack your head I can call for help," John joked.

"Listen, I am the cautious one, remember? Just don't get hurt. I don'twant to have to rescue your ass," I replied.

We both laughed with the wind in our face. An hour passed. The water was now rough enough to make relaxing nearly impossible. We used our paddles laid across both boats to steady ourselves in the swells that now were maybe seven feet high. I pointed out to sea, saying, "Looks really rough out there. Seems like the wind is whipping up the water a lot more than here."

"As long as it stays farther out we are fine. I still feel comfortable in this stuff. It's invigorating."

After two hours into our paddle I could see the rock gardens up ahead and I began to get a little nervous. It was a foreboding kind of nervousness, no doubt due to the fact that the wind had increased to about thirty knots, with the water choppier than ever. The conditions were such that keeping our boats close together and talking became difficult. John was in the lead and seemed hell bent on maintaining a brisk pace. We would ride up the face of a swell and get blasted by the wind, which sent an icy cold spray of salt water into our faces. Then we would drop down into the trough of the swell and couldn't see anything except blue water, until the boat rose back up to the top again, where you got a quick view of what was up ahead.

John was out in front now; three or four swells away from my position. I could hear him hoop and holler as he reached the top of each wave. He seemed to be having a great time. I tried to relax and have fun too, but my gut feeling said that our margin of safety was fast eroding.

Rising high on the swell I could see the rocks and part of the reef looming up ahead. I wondered if John had spotted them too. I leaned into the wind and paddled harder, hoping to catch him before we were into the rock garden area. As I paddled toward the next wave, it suddenly broke sending a cascade of foam and water into my bow and over me. The force picked up the front of the boat and turned it sideways. Within a fraction of a second I was under the water, upside down. I could feel the powerful water pushing my kayak around. With my knees still braced up against the inside of the kayak, I waited until the wave passed over me and then I rolled up. With the combination of a low tide and big wind, the swells could suddenly break without warning.

On the next high wave I looked to see where John was. I spotted him far ahead. He was ignoring one of the cardinal rules of kayaking—*know where your paddling partners are at all times.* He no doubt never saw me go over, nor did he realize how far ahead he was. With the wind in my face there was no way to call him. I swore at the waves, the wind, and John's lack of judgment, and at myself for this predicament we found ourselves in. What started out as a mild risk and a fun paddle had deteriorated into a tough one in heavy seas.

I paddled furiously to catch up to John, narrowly missing being tossed over two more times. The wind was so strong I had to keep my paddle low, my head down and a sharp eye out for breaking waves.

I knew John had a reckless streak, but this was no time to express it. I flashed back to the time when he paddled into a sea cave ignoring my advice to do a wave count before committing to entering the narrow cave opening. Just as he got deep inside a large wave sent white water rushing in. Paddling backwards to exit out, a drenched and yelling John said that he actually hit his helmet on the roof of the cave when it got flooded. He thought that was too much fun. Another time he wanted to kayak-surf the wake of one of the speedy ferries that streaked across the bay. He misjudged the ferry's speed and almost got run over. The passengers thought he was playing a game of chicken with the ferry.

I could feel my muscles tiring as I did a flat out sprint. I reached the crest of a wave and looked to see John dangerously close to the rocks now. I had no choice but to head that way too. Rising up on each wave I got a view that looked increasingly bad. John was now turned toward the open ocean, no doubt in an attempt to paddle away from the rocks. I was getting closer now and could see waves exploding over the rocks. I could feel the fear creeping in my mouth as it became dry, but I knew I had to stay calm and steady. I crested a wave just in time to see John's boat being lifted up and thrown backwards. Natasha's words sounded in my head, '*something bad is going to happen.*' I shook off the memory.

Nothing is going to happen, and we are going to get out of this, I told myself. My heart sank when I looked again and saw John's boat upside down and banging into the rocks, but I didn't see John. I sprinted up and over the last waves there, but couldn't get close enough to his boat. Waves were now pounding the whole area. I frantically looked for John but didn't see him. He couldn't have been dragged under because he had a life vest on. I couldn't stay where I was either, because sooner or later I would be in the water too. I was hoping and praying that he made it to shore. I turned my bow toward shore and paddled as fast as I could to miss the rocks. Soon a wave picked up the back of my kayak and I began surfing down the wave face. My kayak was too long for this kind of surfing but I did my best to cut right and ride it as far as possible.

It wasn't far enough. Over I went. I didn't even have a chance at Eskimo-rolling the boat right side up. I was knocked out of my kayak with razor sharp, shell-encrusted rocks all around. A wave flung me against a rock tearing at my dry suit; I could feel the cold-water rush in. I swam the best I could with the life vest on and spray jacket, then, out of the corner of my eye I spotted John clinging to a large rock, half out of the water. He wasn't moving but would be sucked up against the rock when the surge went out. It seemed forever until I reached him. Coming closer I could see he had a nasty head wound that was bleeding.

"John! John! Are you okay?" I could barely speak, still out of breath and tired. He didn't respond. I checked his pulse; it was there, but weak. Then I saw that somehow he was being held above the water by a big tangle of kelp.

We were trapped offshore in a jumble of rocks. I

noticed a narrow passage that led through the rock beds. I took hold of John's life vest and pulled with all my strength until he broke free of the kelp. I made for shore doing a crawl stroke on my side as best I could. Soon we were in the channel where the incoming waves had lost most of their force on the rocks farther out.

I dragged John up on shore and collapsed, exhausted. After a few minutes I got up and pulled him farther on to the dry sand. He was still unconscious but breathing. I cursed myself for forgetting the helmets. The gash to his head was deep but the bleeding had stopped. I glanced out to sea and saw that John's boat was being washed to shore. Then I spotted my kayak drifting around in shallow water. I ran to drag it to shore, wanting to retrieve the first aid kit.

After attending to John's head wound, I knew I had to get help fast. He was still unconscious. My waterproof map and the responder should still be on my kayak. I sprinted back to retrieve them, but the daypack with the responder was gone! According to the map a road should be right above us, a little way in from shore. I made sure John was high and dry— as comfortable as I could make him, then climbed a small cliff that overlooked the beach, and headed in the direction I hoped was the road.

I found a road, but it looked deserted, unused. Again I cursed our luck. My mounting anxiety was affecting my ability to think straight. I knew that I had to keep it together, and told myself to sit down and get a clear head. As if he were there, I could hear Fred's words: *"David, if you find yourself unprepared for the unknown, drop out of your head and into your body. Learn to adapt, everything you need is all around you and within you. Stay with your breath, and your frustration will leave you."*

I thought of his words over and over. Yes, what have I learned? Am I now going to act like all that time with Fred was spent for nothing? Had I not learned anything? I closed my eyes and soon became calm and centered. I observed the rhythm of my breath as things became quiet inside. Then, I sent out a mental call for anyone in the area to come here, to bring us help. I visualized the thoughts broadcasting out in a wide arc with the message. With each outward breath I visualized and sent out my message. I could feel the force and energy of it happening.

In what seemed like a short time I heard a truck in the distance, but kept my eyes closed and continued to broadcast. The sound of the truck grew louder. I jumped to my feet and waited till it appeared. A lone woman with a dog pulled up and stopped.

"Are you all right? Is something wrong?" she asked.

"Oh, am I glad to see you! Listen, do you have a phone?"

"Why yes, what's wrong?" she said, holding up her cell phone.

"My friend is seriously hurt down on the beach and I need to get help."

"Just press that button down in the corner and it will ring 911," she said, handing me the phone as she got out of the truck. "I might be able to help. I am a nurse. Here, let me call." She took the phone from my hand and quickly pressed 911. After giving directions to the operator, she retrieved a couple of blankets from her truck. "Lets go," she said.

We found John where I had left him, still unconscious. Her dog followed close behind. "We have to keep him warm till the emergency people arrive. He seems to be in a coma."

She continued her examination for further injuries. We carefully wrapped him in the blankets. Aside from small cuts and scrapes it appeared no bones were broken, but a huge lump was swelling at his temple, having turned black and blue since I left him there on the beach.

The wind had died down a bit, most of it blowing harder further out on the water.

"You should probably get stitches for that leg wound," she said, pointing to my torn dry suit, and the bloody rip in the skin underneath.

I looked down, seeing the deep gash. "Funny, I didn't feel anything until you mentioned it."

"Adrenaline does that. Plus you were thinking of your friend. Where were you paddling to, anyway?" she asked, as she bandaged the cut on my leg.

"We were trying to reach Sandy Beach. It's not far from here," I answered. Suddenly I remembered that Natasha was awaiting our arrival. "In fact my girlfriend is waiting for us to show up, and I know she will be very worried by now."

"First things first. Let's focus on getting your friend to the hospital. I can give you a lift to Sandy Beach."

We heard the wail of sirens in the distance. Before long John was on his way to the emergency room. With the help of a fire truck crew we got the kayaks up to the road where the woman insisted we put them on the back of her truck.

"I am sorry, my name is David," I said, realizing I hadn't even told the woman my name. "I don't know how to thank you . . . "

"I'm Maria, no thanks needed. I feel lucky that I paid attention to my intuition and my best friend."

"Best friend?"

"Yes, Zach my black lab. When I ignored my first intuitive thought that I should drive down the road, he began to get excited and wouldn't calm down. He kept barking out the back of the truck. I stopped and got out, asking him what was wrong. I know Zach. He has a keen sense of what's on my mind. "Zach, what is it?" I asked. He kept looking back toward the road we had just passed and barking. Then it dawned on me—the intuitive hit I had about going down that abandoned road! He had picked up on my thought and knew that something was down there.

I told him, "Okay Zachy-boy, let's go find out why you're so nervous!"

"Wow, that's amazing, I said. "I do believe animals know a lot more than we humans can grasp."

"Yes, I find that their antenna is always up, receiving much more than humans do. If we tune into them they will not only inform us, but also teach us about our-selves. They are always present. Not to change the subject, but I work at the same hospital where they are taking John. I need to be reporting for work soon. I'll call to say I've been delayed. Now let's get you back to your girl-friend."

On the drive to Sandy Beach I told Maria about sending my thoughts out for help. "I also believe that's how it works," she said. "My intuition has always been right on, if I listen to it. John is lucky that you knew what to do. We aren't alone in this world, I guess. We are con-nected by thought."

Maria looked to be in her thirties. She was attrac-tive, with a seemingly calm disposition—self assured, competent. It was a godsend that she happened to be driving by.

"Are you married?" I asked.

"No. Never met the right guy, I guess. The men I've met have been too unreliable and not serious enough about what they do in life. That's why I chose nursing. You have to be dedicated and present, not daydreaming about something else you'd rather be doing. I love my work. We get back what we put in."

"I am so glad you happened to be driving by, Maria. I hope someday you find a man that is good enough for you."

As we drove up to Sandy Beach, I spotted my truck with Natasha in it.

"David!" she yelled, "I've been worried sick!" She jumped down from the truck and ran up to me. "Where's

John?"

With teary eyes I told her what had happened. "I want you to meet the angel that came out of nowhere," I said, introducing Maria.

"You have a special man here, intuitively gifted," Maria said.

"Yes, I know. Thank you so much for helping us."

I think that's what life is about, helping one another."

Natasha and I followed Maria to the hospital. We were told that John was stable but still in a coma. It was too early to tell what his future was. The doctor said that he was lucky he hadn't drowned. The seaweed must have saved him.

Maria gave us her phone number, saying she would make sure John had the best of care.

"I'm sorry I didn't listen to you this morning. I didn't hear the subtle warning," I told Natasha.

"You can't change what's done, but you can change what the future brings."

I called John's parents. By the time they arrived at the hospital, it was late. Natasha and I were very tired. Natasha said she would drive. I slept most of the way.

We drove to the hospital, staying nearby through the next three days and nights. When John's parents arrived, Natasha and I went home. Maria was a constant visitor also, as John lay suspended between life and death. She whispered to him that he had spent enough time chasing after pretty angels on the other side. It was time to come back. I told her to call me if anything at all changed. On the fifth day she called, "David, he's back!"

Natasha and I broke speed limits getting to the hospital. John was chatting with Maria when we came in.

"John! I love you buddy, welcome back!"

John just gave a big smile and sort of nodded his head. He was still weak, not completely himself. I gave him a big hug and told him when he was ready, Natasha and I would take him out for all the lobster he could eat.

Maria told us he still had swelling of the brain, and that it was best for him to remain quiet and comfortable. The doctors gave him a good chance of a full recovery if the swelling went down.

John's parents came in, his mother going to his side immediately.

"You guys should have known better! You could have both been killed out there," his father said in a terse voice.

"You're right Mr. Fleming. It was bad judgment on my part. We had no business being out there. I am sorry."

He pushed past me and joined his wife. Maria smiled at me and shook her head. I whispered that we'd be back tomorrow. Then we left, so John could be alone with his parents.

On the way back I thanked Natasha for being so understanding, saying I was sorry that our time together had been so stressful.

"Do you know how I see it?" she resonded. "I see situations as an opportunities to use what I know to be true. Life isn't about disappointment for me anymore. It's about responding with my heart to what life brings me. It's the only way I can live an authentic life," she answered.

Her words sank in. The more time I knew her, the more wisdom I saw she possessed. I told her that, when I was under the stress of the accident, I got angry and had a difficult time staying calm. Responding from my heart wasn't an option I had at that time.

"We always have a choice but you have to realize, if you haven't already, that the thoughts we have affect how our bodies react to any given situation. That can limit our choices."

"I just need more training, I guess."

"You need to observe more—to understand how your mind works. Everyone has certain tendencies in the way they react to life. That comes from our conditioning. But as you know, we are also born with a blueprint for this life, and if we don't follow its design then we follow our conditioned self. While you might become angry when you are fearful, another person might shut down and become passive. We all have a tendency to think certain thoughts out of habit. Notice how your thoughts affect what your body does. Think of your favorite food and your saliva glands start running. Think of making love and your body will start preparing."

"So if just a thought can trigger a body response, how do we control what we think?" I asked.

"By keeping the mind occupied in the present moment. Look, the Tibetans have their mantras and mallow beads, the Catholics have their rosaries, but everyone

211

has their breath. Stay in touch with that and you are always present."

"How is it possible to always be thinking of your breath coming and going?"

"Practice."

John's swelling went down and he was released from the hospital two weeks later. He was told to take it easy for a while and to not strain himself. He started to look and behave like the old John that I knew.

"John, come by this Friday for dinner. Natasha said she would fix one of your favorites— fresh salmon," I said over the phone.

"All right, I'll bring the wine."

Before Friday I got a call from John asking if it was all right if he brought someone along for dinner.

"Of course, anyone I know?"

"You might be surprised. I will leave it at that."

When I answered the door, John was hiding someone behind him. "Surprise!" he laughed.

"Hello David," Maria said, stepping out from behind John.

"Maria! This is a wonerfful," I said, giving her a welcome hug. "Natasha, guess who's here?"

By the time dinner was ready we had already heard all about their new romance.

"Guess I need to be in a coma to make a good impression," John laughed. "You did say some day I would find the woman of my dreams, David. I guess I had to go to the dream world to find her. Your intuition was right on."

Maria said she had felt the connection the moment she saw him, even in his critical state.

"Remember you said that you hoped I would meet a good man? Little did I know it would be your best friend!"

At dinner, I asked John what the last thing was he remembered, before going unconscious.

"I remember my kayak being knocked over by a wave and trying to recover, but I missed two tries at rolling up, so I popped out. The next thing I remember was hitting something really hard."

"That's all you remember? What about when you were in the coma?"

"Nada—although I faintly recall someone saying to stop chasing pretty angels," John said. We all laughed out loud.

By the end of the evening I could see they were a good match. She would be a spiritual inspiration for John. It was clear she possessed a wisdom he needed.

Before they left, John asked when we were going kayaking again. "I think you had better ask your nurse about that!" I said.

"He's right, and for now you can just put that idea out of your mind. It's the straight and narrow for awhile!" Maria answered for him.

It was a week later that Natasha and I went out to dinner, this time in a safe, well-lit area, parking in the restaurant parking lot.

After ordering and relaxing with a glass of wine, I brought up the subject of the Death Mask. I asked

Natasha if she thought the so-called death mask was a warning for me, or if it had anything to do with John's accident.

"The strong intuitive feeling I had, right before you two paddled out, wasn't about either of you specifically. But I knew something was wrong."

"Why didn't I receive an intuitive warning," I wondered.

"I imagine you were too focused on getting ready for your adventure. If you had taken time to sit with the idea awhile, and asked your inner self if it was a good idea, things might have been different."

"It's funny, but my very first impression when John mentioned going was, no way, it gets too crazy out there this time of year. My tendency to want to please my friend over rode my initial thought."

"As I've said before, if we remain outside the present moment, we miss the guidance that is always available."

As she spoke, an overwhelming feeling of love for her enveloped me. I knew that she was the woman I wanted to be with for the rest of my life. I reached over and took her hand. "Will you move back here and live with me? I don't want you to leave. I love you."

"I love you too, but are you sure? When the honeymoon is over, are you still going to want me? Will you love me when I'm old and gray?" she smiled.

"Natasha, I think about you all the time. When you are old and grey, I'll love you just as much, but not as often!"

She smiled and I continued, "You are a wonderful teacher in my life. We will help each other grow and learn."

"I am not looking for a relationship, I am still searching for myself. But I think about you all the time. I really love your energy. It feels good to be near you. I just can't give you an answer right now. I must find my own direction before I support our direction. Can you understand?"

I did understand, but I felt disappointed.

"So how much time do you need? Isn't your direction the same as mine? We both want the same thing don't we?"

"If we are destined to live this life out together, what is your hurry?"

"Have you thought about having children?" I inquired.

"You've been thinking a lot about this, haven't you? You know I'm learning to trust in the moment, to recognize what it tells me, and right now what it tells me is—to stay true to each other and not rush into any decisions. Wait and hear the wisdom inside."

I could see she was right. I was looking for some kind of emotional satisfaction. I tried something else. I planted a kiss on her lips. "Okay then, we will stay true to ourselves and see what happens."

"I love you," she said.

✻CHAPTER SIXTEEN

Natasha would be leaving in a week. I wanted to achieve the technique of consciously leaving my body so that I could visit her and Fred whenever I needed. She told me that she would try the same. Each night we both said that we'd practice the "look at your hands" while dreaming, to see if it worked. I thought she would be the first to achieve it, but soon I had a breakthrough.

While dreaming I found myself at the seashore. I was pointing toward something. Suddenly my awareness locked onto my outstretched hand. "Look at your hands, look at your hands," I heard a voice say.

I held up my hands, and as soon as I looked at them, my dreamlike consciousness leaped into full awareness. *Wow!* I said to myself, *It finally happened. I was out of my body!*

I noticed that it was nighttime, so I looked around to get my bearings. I was at a place I knew well, a place where I had often kayaked. I thought about my apartment and Natasha, and instantly I was in my room where I saw myself and Natasha sleeping.

I was so excited that I giggled to myself. How

strange to see yourself (or should I say, see your body) sound asleep. I moved closer and wanted to reach out and touch Natasha, but hesitated, I didn't know what effect that would have. I wondered if she was off somewhere in a dream and if could I find her. I told myself that I wanted to locate her. But I just remained there. Perhaps she was in deep sleep and indeed in her body. I walked around the apartment and noticed that I could just walk straight through the walls. It was the strangest sensation. I spotted a picture of Fred on the table and thought of visiting him. In an instant things became blurry and the next thing I knew, I was in a mountainous area. It was day time. I looked around and saw the same stone huts where Fred had been before.

"Fred!" I exclaimed, as he walked out of the hut and stopped. Then, as if he sensed something, he looked around slowly in all directions, finally breaking into a big smile. I went to give him a hug but ended up walking right through him!

"Welcome David, congratulations, I see you have finally learned to get out of the constraints of your body."

I didn't hear him in the usual sense and he didn't move his lips. I understood what he said telepathically.

"Fred, can you see me? I am right next to you."

"I am in my physical form, so no, I can't see you, but we are communicating through thought forms."

"Yes I know, but I saw you smile at me."

"I sensed your presence and knew that you were here."

"Amazing! What do you do here?"

"I will show you."

He said that he had perfected the technique that Dorge taught him and now could become invisible. He sat down, closed his eyes and became still. Next, I watched in total awe as his body began to shimmer and phase in and out until he was just a glowing, radiant sphere of light.

"How do I look?" he asked.

"Like a luminous egg-shaped being. You seem to be pulsing in and out of some kind of energy field," I replied.

"Yes, while my physical body is asleep. What you are seeing is an astral body. You appear as an egg shape too, but you still believe you look like yourself

"But I saw my hand in the dream."

"You still think that you have the body that you know so well? Take a closer look."

I tried to look down at my legs but they weren't there, in fact I couldn't see any part of "me".

"You're still trying to see with what you think are your physical eyes. Look with your inner eye."

"How do I do that?"

Fred said to come closer. I then experienced a surge of energy shoot through my forehead, or what I thought was my forehead. "Now look down at your body with the place I just touched," he said.

I looked and saw that I was nothing more than a luminous glow similar to Fred, yet different. Then I noticed everything all around me looked different. I saw the energy within the natural world, similar to what I had ex perienced when I "saw" from my sensing spot inside my physical body.

Fred said to look in the direction of the mountains nearby, along the path leading away from his place.

Fred's hut was on a small flat piece of ground, just off a well-used path. All around were high mountains with a pass that was the only way in and out. I looked in the direction he said, and noticed three other stone huts farther up the trail. I stared at them and then saw two bright, whitish glows slowly moving around inside the huts. I was looking right through the stonewalls of the huts.

"What are those glowing things inside? Are they people?"

"Yes, my neighbors. Now you are seeing rightly. People are no more than energy forms within their physical bodies. One day you just might discover that we are only a single point of light, rather than what you are experiencing now."

As I observed the two forms, I saw the colors change slightly, as well as the intensity. I asked Fred what that meant.

"Our emotions not only affect the physical body but the inner energy form as well. The stronger the emotion the more intense the outpouring of energy."

My contact with Fred was suddenly shaken and with a jolt I woke up.

Natasha woke up too. "David, what's wrong?" she asked. "You were muttering in your sleep and moving around a lot."

It took me a few seconds to get my bearings and realize I was back in my bed. "Natasha, I did it, I was with Fred in Tibet and we had this amazing conversation."

"Oh . . . that's great . . . you woke me up . . ."

"I'm sorry I disturbed you."

"Tell me about it in the morning," she said, and rolled over.

I lay awake recalling everything in the dream. I closed my eyes and tried to go back, but ended up falling asleep.

"Where did you say you were last night?" Natasha asked over breakfast.

"I told you, I finally saw my hands in my sleep and woke up inside my dream. I could see you and myself asleep in bed. Then I went and visited Fred."

"What was it like?"

"It was a feeling of total freedom. It seemed just as real as this. Fred showed me how to see with my inner eyes. He said I still believed that I was in a physical body, even though I knew that I had left it behind."

"I am jealous, but I'll keep trying. Then maybe we could travel together."

"Exactly! Can you imagine how fantastic it might be?"

Even though it worked one time, I couldn't do it again for another two weeks. By then Natasha had gone back to Bella Namu. We had a tearful goodbye and promised to stay in touch. I told her to keep practicing, so that we could visit each other.

I decided to practice in the copper room where nothing would disturb me. As before, as soon as I looked at my hands I "woke up" on the other side. This time I tried to visit Natasha.

I found myself in the Raven's Nest. Helen and Natasha were busy with customers. It was the strangest thing I had ever experienced. There I was looking at everyone, and no one knew that I was there. Like a kid left home alone, I decided to have some fun.

A man and woman were having dinner. They were a heavy set couple in their fifties. I went over and sat down in the middle of their table facing the man, and listened in on their conversation. He was complaining about the slow fishing season and said they should move to Seattle where there was more work. She said what he needed to do was stop complaining and work with a better crew.

I spun around and faced her. She chastised him for working with a crew that did nothing but drink. No wonder they didn't catch fish!

As they argued, I had a thought that maybe I could "will" something to move, like in the movie "Ghost" I had seen so long ago. I decided to move her plate of food. Nothing happened so I put out an imaginary hand and tried moving energy through it as I did in the physical world. Still no movement. Finally I just thought of the plate moving in front of her. I gasped as I saw it move, even though it was only an inch or so. They didn't seem to notice, so I thought once again of the plate of food moving. All at once the plate moved about four inches.

"Did you see that!" the man said excitedly, pointing over at her plate.

"See what? Now, don't change the subject, just because you know I am right."

"I ain't changing nothing. Your plate just moved!"

"That's it! You're not drinking another drop. Waitress can we have our bill?" she called out.

Natasha came over, "Jean, is something the matter?"

"Yes, Bill here is hallucinating, and I am cutting off his alcohol."

"Natasha, I swear I just saw that plate move across the table. She won't believe me," he said.

I tried to will my thoughts to Natasha: "Natasha, I did it, I am right here."

She acted like she didn't receive anything until she gave them their bill and started to walk away. She stopped for a moment and turned back, looking towards the table. Then she shook her head and walked on.

The couple continued arguing back and forth.

Okay, I thought. I'll make a believer out of her. I focused my thoughts the best I could, and to my surprise the plate slid right off the table and into the woman's lap.

"Good God, Bill! What's going on!!" she said. Almost hysterically, she jumped up from the table, leaving the plate to slip out of her lap, spilling food and breaking on the floor. I burst out laughing. Of course no one could hear me.

"I told you it moved!" the man quipped. "Now

let's get out of here!"

They rushed for the door, throwing two twenties down on the table. Helen came over and cleaned up the mess.

'Some people! she thought to herself.

Next, I swished over to the bar and listened in on two younger men's conversation. They were talking about women, saying what a bitch they could be. "You spend all your money on them and they still act like you owe them."

"I know, like we can never be good enough. It pisses me off sometimes," the other one said.

Natasha came over. "Are you two going to order anything to eat?" she asked.

"Naw, I wouldn't want to spoil my beer high," one of them said. Natasha walked away.

"I wouldn't mind eating her," one said laughing.

"Got that right, I could screw her till the cows come home," the other said, bursting into laughter.

This angered me and I decided to teach them a lesson. After I calmed down I concentrated on moving their pitcher of beer on the counter. It moved slightly. Again I focused my thoughts. The pitcher turned over, spilling its contents onto the two men. They jumped to their feet and accused each other of spilling the beer.

"Damn it! Hey, bartender, we need another pitcher."

After receiving another pitcher of beer and towels to wipe themselves off, they resumed their rude remarks. I wanted them out of there. They weren't going to sit there and talk about Natasha that way!

Setting my sights on the fresh pitcher of beer, I succeeded a second time in drenching them. "What the hell is going on!" one of them said out loud.

"Hey, that's it for you two. You're out of here," the bartender barked.

"What! The stupid beer just flew off the bar." "Right—now take your wet asses out of here or you'll have more to worry about than spilt beer."

The two men made a noisy exit, cursing and muttering under their breaths.

"What is going on tonight?" Helen asked to no one in particular as she mopped up their mess. I felt sorry for Helen having to clean up the mess I was responsible for, but I was having a ball. I knew my newfound freedom was probably going over the line, but those two deserved it.

I looked around the room. A couple was at the pool table. I sat down on the side of the pool table and watched them taking practice shots. He was a much better player than she was, and seemed to take pride in showing off. He was a big burly man in his forties. She was in her thirties, about average size. She looked like she might be Native American, with black hair and high cheekbones. He boasted that he could beat anyone in town, so just to make things fair he would give her two shots for his one.

"I can play just like everyone else, you don't need to make it easy," she told him.

"You don't stand a chance honey. Who do you

think you're playing against, some rookie?" he answered, slamming a ball in the corner pocket.

"Just the same, I play by the rules, I am no different," the woman responded.

"Suit yourself," he replied, racking up the balls for a new game.

I couldn't help myself. I would even up the odds and better yet, trim off some of his pride.

He rocketed the cue ball into the racked group, scattering them around the table, leaving two balls in inside pockets. He made shot after shot until he had only two balls left besides the eight ball.

He missed his next shot. Now it was her turn—except she didn't have a straight in shot anywhere. I saw that she wanted to run a ball down to the corner pocket, so I waited there and focused my energy on the ball rolling in. It did. Next, she needed to bank a shot into the side pocket. "We" sank that one too. By the time she sank her fifth ball, her suitor was getting nervous. The cigar he was chewing on was flickering back and forth at a rapid pace, and his eyes were bulging out of their sockets.

"We" missed the next shot. He quickly sank two more balls and was now down to just the eight ball in order to win the game. He lined up the shot and I did my best to make it miss the hole. He cursed himself as his ball nearly went in. He stood nervously rubbing chalk on the cue stick, chewing his cigar, eyes darting about the table.

She/we played well and were now down to one ball, the final eight ball. She had a tricky shot to make.

The ball had to bank off two cushions before finding its home in the end pocket. We didn't get the second bank right, and it was now his turn. I foiled his effort, sending him into a tongue-tied, stammering ego of disbelief.

The eight ball was at the end of the table near the side. She had to just kiss the side of the eight ball and roll it in the end pocket, winning the game. She took her time checking the angle. He was beside himself, pacing back and forth, his face flushed.

The cue ball rolled slowly down the table, just brushing up against the eight ball, which sent it rolling and dropped it right into the end pocket.

"Oh my God, I don't believe it!" she said, "So you're the best in town, huh?"

She had beaten him!

He was still staring at the corner pocket, wondering if he just got hustled. Finally he acknowledged her triumphant win.

"Okay, I take it back. You're one hell of a player!"

I was as enthralled as she was in winning the game. I looked around the room and suddenly remembered Natasha, but didn't see her. Then I noticed someone sitting at a corner table, head down. I couldn't see the face. I took a double take at the shape sitting there—he or she seemed to be glowing. I moved closer to get a better view.

"Care for a game of pool," the shape said.

"Dorge!!! What–why are you here?"

"Why are you here?" he responded.

"I can't believe it. How did you find me?"

"By now you should know that you can't hide—even in the vast universe. I came to check up on you."

"How long have you been here?" I asked.

"Oh, I saw the antics that so amused you."

I didn't know what to say. To me I was just having fun, exploring the possibilities of my newfound abilities.

"With increased powers come increased responsibilities," Dorge said. "With ultimate power comes ultimate responsibility. You can't have it both ways. It's only the false sense of self that thinks so."

"But I meant no harm. In fact those two guys deserved what they got," I protested.

"David, go back and think deeply about what I said." He slapped his hands together with a loud whack and I woke up. I felt groggy and off center. I left the room and went to sit down at John's workbench.

I thought through the whole thing, and knew that I probably should not have played the games I did, even if I felt justified. My intention was to go and see Natasha but I got distracted. I lost my chance to see her!

The more I thought about it the more agitated I became with myself for having been so foolish. I got up and walked around the studio feeling pissed off. My anger increased until I slammed my fist into a wall, punching a hole in the sheet rock. I continued to walk around the room, mad as hell, until I realized that my ego had got the best of me. I was out of control. I had lost my center and my focus. I had taken both for granted.

I sat down and closed my eyes, trying to calm my mind and find my center. It took a long time before I felt like the storm had passed. How had I wandered so far in such a short time? I looked at the damage I did to John's wall. The wall could be fixed easy enough, but I would need more correcting. Could it be that the energy level that I had attained was channeled through my anger?

When I lived with Fred, I could check in and get guidance whenever I needed, but now I was alone and needed to be careful of letting negative thoughts take hold. I didn't sleep well that night, I woke up tired and in a sour mood. Why didn't Natasha want to live with me? And why was I trying to develop all these powers anyway? What about my life, my work—the easygoing life I had before I went off to learn to carve. Of course I knew the answers, but my mind refused to give in to reason.

It seemed like my life somehow had come to a halt, and was suddenly stale. I began to question everything.

I didn't see much of John any more because he stayed with Maria at her place near the coast. I was happy for him, but I didn't have that many close friends that I cared to hang out with. Besides, they weren't into what I was obsessed with. I felt myself falling into a blue funk and knew that it was my mind and not my spirit that was responsible. I told myself that I needed to meditate and practice more. For the first time, in a long time, I felt isolated and lonely. I had lost my edge and the sense of magic that I had taken for granted ever since I came back from Fred's. I needed to make contact with him again, but I wasn't having any success getting out of my body again. Something was wrong, but I didn't know what it was. My work in photography started to suffer. I had taken too much time off from my clients, and a few began using other photographers.

I realized that I needed to be back with Fred, Dorge, and Natasha. I had experienced realities and a glimpse of a life that I knew was the direction I needed to go. I never realized just how strong my ego, my false self, really was, until it was challenged by a greater purpose. I had experienced my true inner self, my own particular blueprint for this life, and I wasn't going to throw it all away.

I had called The Raven's Nest a few times to catch Natasha at work but each time she wasn't there. It wasn't easy getting through. The phone seemed to be out of service sometimes. I decided to try again.

"Who do you want to speak to?"

"Natasha, is she there?"

"Hello, this is Natasha."

"Natasha! It's David. Finally you're there. How are you?"

"Oh, it's good to hear your voice! You sound different. Are you okay?"

"Let's just say my mind has been stalking me, but I am fine really. I'm thinking of coming up to see you. I need to connect. I am going nuts down here. I can't seem to stay connected."

"Didn't you get my letter yet?"

"No, when did you send it?"

"A week ago. It must have taken a detour. Don't make a decision to come up here till you read it. If you don't get it by next week, let me know."

"Is something wrong? You don't want me to visit?"

"I do, but just read the letter first. You might be surprised."

We talked awhile and then she had to get back to work.

It was two more days before her letter showed up. My life went from dark and cloudy to bright and sunny in just ten words: *"Why don't you move up here and live with me?"* the letter read!

I reread those ten words over and over. She said that I could stay with her and be close to Fred when he came back from Tibet. She wondered if I could support myself once I arrived. What would I do with my photography work? In essence she had decided that living together was something she wanted, after giving it much thought. She was waiting to hear from me.

I wasted no time calling back to tell her how happy I was. I had to get a lot of things in order, and said it would be several days, maybe a couple weeks before I could be ready. Of course the reality of what I was doing sank in quickly. I might have to stop photography altogether, and find some other line of work. I would be entering a whole new life . . . but then I thought, haven't I already entered it?

The days flew by as I made arrangements. I was amazed how much stuff I had acquired, and held onto over the years, that no longer had a place in my life. I gave away, sold, and donated things I no longer needed. I made way for a new life, one that honored the spirit more than the material.

I told Natasha over the phone that I would be moving up in another week. She told me that she had the strongest, intuitive feeling that Fred was back, but that she hadn't seen or heard from him.

"It's funny you said that, I've been thinking a lot about him recently, and I keep getting a feeling that he is near."

I was in the midst of packing when I got a phone call. "David, hello. This is Paul down at the Gallery. A friend of ours is here and wants to see you."

"Oh really, who might that be?" I replied, surprised to hear from Paul, whom I hadn't seen for some time.

"It's a surprise, come on down."

I dropped what I was doing and drove to the gallery.

I was greeted by Paul. He took me to the back room where I had last seen Dorge, and there was Fred!

"Fred!" I shouted, "I thought you were . . ."

"I was, but I'm here now. My you're looking a little rough around the edges—neglecting your practice, are you?" he said smiling.

"Yes, I'm afraid I was experiencing a good dose of my false self. Guess what I'm doing though?"

Fred rubbed his chin, pondering my question. "Ahhh . . . Let's see . . . you've packed your things and are ready to continue on the path."

"How did you know!"

"You didn't really think I would put you upon a

new path and not make sure you could walk it. I've been keeping my eye on you, and now I think it is time for you to go further into your own mystery."

"You don't know how happy I am to see you, Fred. As soon as I made up my mind to go live with Natasha, it felt like I got my life back."

He laughed and slapped his thigh.

"You never lost it, you just misplaced it for a while. Happens to all of us now and then!"

It felt so wonderful to be with Fred. I realized how much I had missed him and his wisdom. He said that he would be returning to Tibet for a brief spell, before coming back up North. He looked forward to seeing me in Bella Namu. I told him about the death mask and John's close call with death.

"Death calls sometimes, not to take us, but to get our attention, to remind us to make the most of the life we have. The mask wasn't just about you, or John, but about everyone—anyone who lives behind a false sense of who they think they are. We are beings of light, consciousness and love. When we finally surrender to that, we surrender the mask."

Three days later, eager to be with Natasha, I left Seattle for Bella Namu.

Fred came to see me off at the ferry dock. As the ferry pulled away from the terminal, he stood there, waving me on. It was not *good-bye* that his gesture was saying to me. It was *bon voyage!*

I sat back and looked out the window, as the ferry pulled away from the dock. Moonlight was dancing on the water, creating a silvery path that stretched far and wide across dark distances. I saw the reflection of my face in the window. I noticed that if I chose to see my reflection in the window, I could not focus on the moonlight dancing on the water.

I realized that life was like that. We could choose to focus on our image, or we could look beyond ourselves to marvel at the magic of it all, seeing the Divine Spirit we can all embody.